Gorilla-shaped .... ir
ancestors like cordwood in the living room . . .

A throwback planet of duelling masters where
huge poisonous bats rule the sky and serpents the
size of semi-trailers slither through rotting
jungle . . .

An immortal race of sarcastic mansized beetles
who swear like longshoremen and move their planet
by collective thought to improve the weather . . .

Worlds of unimaginable danger and splendor were an
everyday reality for Otto McGavin, undercover agent
for the all-powerful Confederación. Assassinate a pres-
ident? Sterilize a planet? Nothing was too vicious in his
line of work. And when it came to searing laser murder,
Otto was one of the best—he had to be, to survive. But
whenever he returned to Earth, and the personality
overlays were peeled away, he tried desperately to believe he could stop killing . . .

Only Joe Haldeman could bring such depth of vision to
this story of an idealistic Anglo-Buddhist trained to be
one of the most cool-nerved killers in the universe.

Other Avon books by
Joe Haldeman

MINDBRIDGE
STUDY WAR NO MORE

ALL MY SINS REMEMBERED

JOE HALDEMAN

AVON
PUBLISHERS OF BARD, CAMELOT, DISCUS AND FLARE BOOKS

The stories "To Fit the Crime" and "The Only War We've Got" appeared in rather different form in *Galaxy* magazine: Copyright © Universal Publishing and Distribution Corp., 1971, 1974.

Illustration by Michael Whelan

AVON BOOKS
A division of
The Hearst Corporation
959 Eighth Avenue
New York, New York 10019

First Avon Printing, November, 1978

AVON TRADEMARK REG. U.S. PAT. OFF AND IN
OTHER COUNTRIES, MARCA REGISTRADA,
HECHO EN CANADA

Printed in Canada

UNV 12 11 10 9 8 7 6 5

For Gordy Dickson:
Sculptor,
   Weaver,
      Jolly tinker.

CONTENTS

INTERVIEW: Age 22   9

PROLOGUE   12

REDUNDANCY CHECK: Age 32   21

EPISODE: To Fit the Crime   25

REDUNDANCY CHECK: Age 39   87

EPISODE: The Only War We've Got   91

REDUNDANCY CHECK: Age 44   153

EPISODE: All My Sins Remembered   157

INTERVIEW: Age 45   218

INTERVIEW:
AGE 22

Close your eyes.
All right.
Do you feel anything?
No.
Good. Open your eyes. State name, age, relief number.
Otto McGavin. Age 22. 8462-00954-3133.
Why do you desire a position with the Confederación?
I want to go places and do things. I have never left
Earth. This is the most interesting way to do it. I be-
lieve in the Confederación, and want to help it protect
the rights of humans and nonhumans.
Do the initials TBII mean anything to you?
No.
*To protect the rights of humans and nonhumans,
would you lie, cheat, steal, and kill?*
I . . . I'm an Anglo-Buddhist.
If enough depended on it, would you kill?
I don't know. I don't think so.
Relax.
—McGavin finds himself walking down an alley in a
strange city. There's a small hard lump to the right of
the small of his back. He checks; it's a laser pistol.
While it's still in his hand, a figure jumps out of the
shadows. "All yer money, cob," he says. McGavin fires
instinctively, killing him.

9

Would you do that?

I don't know. I think I would. And feel remorse, and wish his soul—

Relax.

—The same alley, in shadow. Two men standing under a dim light ahead of him. One holds a knife. "Just chuck it over, an' you won't be hurt." Otto shoots the brigand in the back, killing him.

Would you do that?

I don't think so. I would wait and see whether he actually intended to harm the man . . . and would first give him a chance to surrender.

Relax.

—The same alley. Otto is peering into a window, laser in hand. Inside, a man sits drinking tea and reading. Otto's assignment is to assassinate him. He aims carefully and shoots the man in the head.

Would you do that?

No.

Very well. Inkblot. Nail file. Soup. Fandango.

Otto shook his head and looked at the clock on the office wall. "That didn't take long," he said.

"Rarely does," the interviewer said. An attendant unstuck the electrodes pasted to Otto's head, arms, and chest, and then left.

Otto slipped back into his shirt. "Did I pass?"

"Well, this is not the sort of test you 'pass'." He took a sheet of paper off the top of Otto's application packet and slid it across the desk. "Please initial the 'Interview Completed' box.

"There are various positions you're undoubtedly eligible for. Whether there are openings, that's another question."

He stood to go. "How soon will I find out?"

"Two or three days." They shook hands and Otto left. The interviewer touched his ear, activating a communicator, and recited a sequence of numbers.

"Hello, Rafael? Just finished with that McGavin kid. Maybe you can use him." He paused, listening.

"Well, his training, academic training, is appropriate. Politics and economics, subarea in xenosociology. Physical condition superb. Megathlon winner, reflexes like a cat. The only problem I see is attitudinal; he's a little too idealistic. Religious."

He laughed. "We certainly can. I'll have the tapes sent up. Endit."

There was hope for McGavin, he thought. In the second situation, he'd said he would give the man a chance to surrender . . . not a chance to get away.

PROLOGUE

Two years later:

Otto walked slowly along the broken slidewalk that overlooked the East River, enjoying the autumn breeze and the tang of ozone from the crawling stream of traffic beneath his feet. Approaching the UM building, he tried to contain his excitement. His first offplanet assignment.

He'd been to the Moon as part of his intensive and confusing training, but that was really just a suburb of Earth. This would be for real.

Georges Ledoux's office was in the subbasement of the building. Getting out of the elevator you stepped through a search ring guarded by two tense armed men. Otto didn't set it off.

The third door down had a small card saying G. Ledoux/Planning. It opened before Otto could knock.

"Come in, Mr. McGavin." The office was a cheerfully cluttered place, piles of paper held down with bric-a-brac from a dozen worlds, a battered wooden desk, soft chairs covered with worn but real leather. Ledoux was a bald, slight man, also leathery, smiling. He motioned Otto to a chair.

"We'll get to your assignment in a minute. First, I'd like to clear up a few things about what you've been doing the past two years. You know that a great deal of your training was under deep hypnosis."

"That was pretty easy to figure out."

"Quite so. Now it's time to bring it up to the surface."
He glanced at a slip of paper in his hand. "Close your
eyes . . . 'atlas, beach ball, mantra, pest.' "

. . . black precipitate of iodine and ammonium hyd-
roxide . . . in the kidney even superficial-seeming wound
brings on shock . . . kick, don't punch . . . go for the
eyes . . . conceal the knife until you're in range . . .
short bursts to preserve power . . . 'fence with your
head, not with your heart' . . . fingers stiff into soft area
under sternum, aim for backbone . . . once he's down
kick his head . . . sell your life, don't give it away . . .

"My God!" Otto opened his eyes.

Ledoux picked up a heavy-bladed knife from his desk
and hurled it straight at Otto's heart. Otto plucked it
out of the air without thinking.

"I . . . I'm not a diplomat at all."

"No. You know enough about it to masquerade as
one. That's all."

"I'm a Class 2 operator for the TBII?"

"That's right. And slated to be a prime operator after
another year."

Otto shook his head, as if to clear it.

"I know," Ledoux said gently. "It's not the cruise you
signed up for."

Otto toyed with the knife. "More interesting, actually.
And more useful."

"We like to think so.

"This first assignment will not require any personality
overlay"—the phrase triggered a memory of two months
of training—"but will be TBII business, nevertheless.
You'll be assisting a prime operator named Susan
Avery, on the planet Depot."

"Arcturus IV," Otto said, with a trace of wonder.

"Yes. She is on the planet as Olivia Parenago, Earth's
ambassador."

"Where is the real Parenago?"

"Dead, murdered. Do you know what a 'protection
racket' is?" Otto shook his head. "Well, it's an obscure

13

term for a specialized kind of blackmail. I come to you and offer not to burn down your place of business, with you inside, for a certain amount of money, paid regularly."

"Sounds like something for the local authorities to take care of."

"Normally, yes. Parenago got involved in it because she suspected it was affecting interstellar commerce— which technically would bring it into our sphere of influence. And the local authorities are evidently corrupt.

"With the murder of an ambassador, of course, there's no question that it's Confederación business. TBII business."

McGavin nodded slowly. "Will I be impersonating anybody?"

"Only yourself. A junior attaché. You'll have to attend various functions, give out medals and plaques, that sort of thing. Mainly, you'll be helping Avery with footwork, research—and violence, if there is any."

"Think there will be?"

He shrugged. "The only ones on the planet who know about the substitution, besides you and Avery, will be the ones who killed Parenago. They killed her brutally."

"You're sure there was more than one?"

"At least three. Two held her arms and legs while the other killed her at leisure."

Depot was a well-developed planet that moved in a tight orbit around Arcturus's invisible companion Sleeper ("real" name TN Bootes AA). Sleeper was the closest tachyon nexus to Earth, so almost every outbound ship stopped at Depot to refuel and take on supplies.

Otto was stationed in Jonestown, the planet's largest city. It had a university and a spaceport and was rougher, raunchier, dirtier, and noisier than any place he had ever been. He liked it.

He was walking with Susan Avery in the industrial park, where they wouldn't be overheard. She was a few years older than he, intelligent and tough if not physically attractive (though there was no way to tell what she really looked like; she was a perfect xerox of Olivia Parenago). She had been a prime operator for five years.

"We may have a new informant," she said.

"Better at staying alive than the last one?"

"We hope." The first informant, a merchant who'd decided to stop paying, had died of an industrial accident during the half-hour that elapsed between his phone call to Parenago and her arrival at his place of business. He'd called the police first. "She's a court recorder in the third district; I met her at a luncheon and she passed me a note. Through some jurisdictional technicality, she has access to police credit records."

"Did she say anything specific?"

"Only that she thought she had evidence of a Charter violation. That would have to be offworld money going into police pockets. Let's go out on the dock. Be sightseers." They were walking along a bay whose shore was dominated by a huge electrolysis plant, churning out oxygen for spaceship resupply and hydrogen for local energy.

They moved to the end of the dock and sat there, watching a mat of purple seaweed lap against the pilings. There was a slight smell of chlorine in the air.

"She didn't want to bring her evidence to Jonestown; didn't want to take it from her office until she knew that she could be far away when the trouble starts."

"Reasonable."

"Sure. So I've got her booked on a two-week industrial sightseeing tour of the Sleeper plants, under a false name. I'll be taking her tickets to her, down in Silica, this afternoon."

15

"Should I come with you?"

"No, I'll be back tonight sometime. What I want you to do is go back to the office and set up an all-contingencies algorithm.

"Look at the city and state tables of organization and figure out how many Confederación administrators, and how much muscle, would be required to take over the police—quickly and, if possible, without bloodshed. Send in an order for them, under my name and with my scramble, to be filled if I don't cancel within twenty-four hours. 'Explanation to follow.' Then get back to your place and lock the door until you hear from me. Clear?"

"I suppose . . . commandos for muscle?"

"Best; keep from wrecking the town. Are you dressed?"

"Uh, no." The shoulder holster had given him a rash.

"Otto." She put a hand on his knee. "I know you're a gentle sort. But you saw what these bastards did to . . . the real Olivia."

He nodded. Having seen a holo on Earth had kept him uncomfortable around Avery for the first few days. Seeing her face made him visualize the mutilated body.

"So go dressed, double-dressed. I want to keep you in one piece." She stood up. "I'd rather not involve any other embassy people in this. Will you need any help with the technical end?"

"No, it's the same kind of machine we used in training." They started walking down the dock. "Should we split up?"

"Not if you're not dressed." She slid a hand lightly under his bicep and moved close to him, falling into step. "Act like we're lovers, out for a stroll," she said in a conspiratorial whisper.

An unsurprisingly easy act. "It won't take you out of your way?"

"Shuttle to Silica won't leave for six hours; gives me plenty of time."

Plenty of time for what, Otto wondered, and subsequently found out. Avery made the shuttle with two minutes to spare.

The computation, coding, and message transmission took Otto until after midnight. Following Avery's advice, he left the embassy through a secret entrance, took a roundabout way home, on foot, and snuck into his apartment via rooftop and service door. The only thing he was really worried about was being arrested as a burglar.

He slept fully dressed and armed, feeling ridiculous, and woke up with a rash. The phone was buzzing.

It wasn't Avery; it was the embassy, wondering where she was. Otto said he didn't know. The man complained that she had appointments all day. Would Otto come in and substitute until Avery showed up? Of course.

He took a direct route to the office and nobody tried to assassinate him. He sat behind Avery's desk for eight hours, being polite to a succession of complainers, trying to find a comfortable position with a heavy-duty Westinghouse weighing down his left side and a small Walther neurotangler in a spring-sheath taped to the small of his back. He buzzed Avery's apartment between interviews, and worried.

When the day was finally over, he hurried directly to Avery's place. Knocked and rang and finally tried to pop the lock. TBII agents know a number of ways to subvert locks, but it works both ways; Avery evidently knew one more trick than Otto did. He considered using the Westinghouse on it, but instead found the supervisor and bullied him into opening it.

Nobody in the living room, but a window was missing, smoothly melted away around the edges. The supervisor demanded to know who was going to pay for it.

He followed Otto around from room to room, demanding, complaining. When Otto opened the bathroom door he smelled something odd, closed his eyes, said a three-word Buddhist prayer, stepped inside, and found Susan Avery lying naked in the tub, face-down in two centimeters of clotted blood.

REDUNDANCY CHECK: AGE 32

Biographical check, please, go:
I was born Otto Jules McGavin on 24 Avril AC 198, on Earth, with jus sanguinus citizenship to
Skip to age 22, please, go:
Thought I was being trained for Confederación xenosociology or diplomacy post but had been with TBII for two years, all the immersion therapy that I couldn't remember, it was weapons and dirty tricks, wondered why the other students always had more to talk about but my counselor said it was normal, I tested out fine under hypnosis, it would all be clear and accessible by graduation, but all through my twenty-second year, I remember, felt like I worked harder than anyone else but
You did, Otto. Skip to age 25, please, go:
I was a Class 2 operator until mid-223, when I went on probationary prime operator status and got my first personality overlay, impersonating Mercurio de Follette, a credit-union manager on Mundo Lagardo suspected of Article Three violation
Was he guilty? Please, go:
Of course he was but we wanted to see which others were implicated, it turned out his whole surrogate-family
Skip to age 26, please, go:
That was the year I killed my first man, third assignment as a prime, it was self-defense in a way, in a way,

21

he had me at his mercy if he only knew, I had to kill
him or he would, in a way it was self-defense
Syzygy.
in a way it was
Aardvark, worship-devil.
self-defense.
Gerund. Now sleep.

EPISODE:

TO FIT THE CRIME

Every direction seems uphill in artificial gravity. Isaac Crowell, Ph.D., paused to get his breath, pushed damp hair back from his forehead, and tapped on the door of the psychiatrist's stateroom. It slid open.

"Ah, Dr. Crowell." The man behind the desk was as thin as Crowell was fat. "Please come in, sit down."

"Thank you." Crowell eased himself into the sturdiest-looking chair. "You, uh, you wanted . . ."

"Yes." The psychiatrist leaned forward and spoke clearly: "Syzygy. Aardvark, worship-devil. Gerund."

Crowell blinked one long slow blink. Then he looked down at the expanse of his belly and shook his head, amazed. He took a thumb and forefingerful of flab and pinched. "Ouch!"

"Good job," the psychiatrist said.

"Wonderful. You couldn't have had the old boy take off some weight first? Before I got stuck in him?"

"Necessary to the image, Otto."

"Otto . . . yes. It comes back, all . . . now. I'm—"

"Wait!" The man pushed a button on his desk and the door whispered shut. "Sorry. Go on."

"I'm Otto McGavin, a prime operator. A prime. For the TBII. And you're no more a psychiatrist than I am a Dr. Isaac Crowell. You're Sam, uh, Nimitz. Used to be a section leader when I was stationed on Springworld."

25

"That's right, Otto—you have quite a memory. I don't think we met more than twice."

"Three times. Two cocktail parties and a bridge game. Your partner had a grand slam and I still haven't figured out how she cheated."

He shrugged. "She was a prime, too."

"'Was,' yeah. You know she's dead now."

"I don't think I'm authorized to—"

"Sure. You my briefing officer this time?"

"That's right." Nimitz pulled a long envelope from an inside cape pocket. He broke the plastic seal and handed it to Otto. "Five-minute ink," he said.

Otto scanned the three pages quickly and then read slowly from beginning to end. He handed it back just as the printing faded.

"Any questions?"

"Well . . . okay, I'm this fat old professor, Crowell. Or will be when you push me back through the mnemonic sequence. Can I speak the language as well as he could?"

"Probably not quite as well. There aren't any learning tapes for Bruuchian; Crowell's the only person who ever bothered to learn a dialect of the language.

"You were under mutual hypnosis with him for five weeks, learning it. Throat sore?"

Otto reached to touch his Adam's apple and recoiled when he hit Crowell's fourth chin. "God, this guy's in lousy shape. Yeah, I feel a little hoarse."

"The language is mostly growls. I learned a stock phrase in it." He made a noise like a tenor rhinoceros in pain.

"What the hell does *that* mean?"

"It's in the dialect you learned, a standard greeting in the informal mode: 'Clouds are not for your family./ May you die in the sun.' Of course, it rhymes in Bruuchian. Everything rhymes in Bruuchian; every noun ends in the same syllable. A protracted belch."

"Wonderful. I'll have laryngitis after a half hour of small talk."

"No. You'll remember once you get back into the Crowell persona. You've got lozenges in your baggage that make it easier on your throat."

"Good." Otto kneaded one enormous thigh. "Look, I hope this job won't call for any action. Must be carrying around my own weight in plastiflesh."

"Very nearly."

"That report said Crowell hadn't been on the planet for eleven years—why couldn't they just say he'd been on a diet?"

"No, you might run into some recent acquaintance. Besides, part of the job requires that you look as harmless as possible."

"I don't mind looking harmless . . . but in 1.2 gees I'm going to *be* harmless! I worked up a sweat walking down the corridor here—in less than one gee. How——"

"We have confidence in you. Otto. You primes always come through in a pinch."

". . . or die trying. Goddamn hypnoconditioning."

"Your own best interests." Nimitz began filling a pipe. "Syzygy. Aardvark. Worship-devil. Gerund."

Otto slumped back in the chair; his next breath was a snore.

"Otto, when I awaken you, you will be about ten per cent Otto McGavin and ninety per cent your artificial personality overlay, Dr. Isaac Crowell. You will remember your mission and all of your training as a prime operator—but your initial reaction to any normal situation will be consistent with Crowell's personality and knowledge. Only in stress situations will your reactions be those of a prime operator.

"Gerund. Devil-worship. Aardvark. Syzygy."

Crowell/McGavin awoke in mid-snore. He pulled himself out of the chair and winked at Nimitz. In Crowell's gravelly voice: "Thank you so much, Dr. Sanchez. The therapy was most soothing."

"Think nothing of it, Dr. Crowell. That's what the ship pays me for."

2

"This is a bloody outrage! Young man—do you know who I am?"

The customs inspector tried to look bored and hostile at the same time. He put Crowell's ID capsule back into the microfiche viewer and stared at it for a long time. "According to this, you're Isaac Crowell, out of Macrobastia, born on Terra. You're sixty and look seventy. That don't get you past the strip-down inspection."

"I demand to see your supervisor."

"Uncheck. Ain't in today. You can wait for him in that little room there. It has a nice lock."

"But you—"

"Ne gonna call my boss his one free day; ne an some shy offworld bloat. You can wait in the room. Ne'll starve."

"Say, now, say." A stocky little man with a headful of shellacked curls strutted over. "What seems to— Isaac! Isaac *Crowell*! What brings you back?"

Crowell clasped the man's hand—his palm damp and warm—and searched artificial memories for a fraction of a second until the face and name clicked into place. "Jonathon Lyndham. So good to see you. Especially now."

"What, there's some kind of trouble?"

"I don't know, Jonathon. This . . . gentleman doesn't want to let me through the turnstile. Not unless I do some sort of a, a striptease."

Lyndham pursed his lips and regarded the inspector. "Smythe. Don't you know who *this man is?*"

"He's . . . no, sah."

"Did you go to school?"

"Yes, sah. Twelve years."

28

"Doctor Isaac Sebastian Crowell." Lyndham reached awkwardly across the barrier and put his hand on Crowell's shoulder. "Author of *Anomaly Resolved*—the book that put this planet on the regular spacelanes."

Actually, the book had sold well enough on Bruuch, and also on Euphrates, where the colonists faced a similar situation with regard to exploiting alien natives; but it was a failure everywhere else. Other anthropologists, while admiring Crowell's tenacity, felt that he'd let sentiment interfere with objectivity. There's an uncertainty principle in field work; it's hard to analyze your subjects if you have too much affection for them.

And as for being on the regular spacelanes, Bruuch had one cargo ship a week, usually late.

"Here, let me see those papers." The clerk gladly handed over the clearance forms. "I'll take full responsibility." He scrawled initials in a dozen places and handed them back. "This is no common tourist—without the influence of his book, you'd be working in the mines. Ne pushing paper once a week."

The clerk pushed a button and the turnstile buzzed. "Let's go, Isaac. The Company'll buy you a drink."

Crowell squeezed through the narrow opening and shuffled after Lyndham to the spaceport bar. The place was furnished with native handcrafts: tables and chairs carved from the dense black ironwood that resembled obsidian more than any other Terran material.

Crowell had difficulty drawing the heavy chair out from under the table. He plopped down into it and wiped his face with an outlandishly large handkerchief.

"Jonathon . . . I don't know if I can handle this gravity. I'm not a young man anymore and . . . well, I've let myself go a little." Ten per cent reminded itself: *I'm thirty-two and in superb physical condition.*

"Oh, you'll get used to it, Isaac. Let me enroll you in our health club—we'll shrink those extra pounds off in no time."

"That would be nice," Crowell said hastily (no

29

amount of exercise will reduce plastiflesh), "but I doubt I'll have the time. My publisher sent me here to gather material for an update of *Anomaly* . . . probably be here a month or less."

"Oh—that's a pity. But I think you'll find that things have changed enough to warrant a longer stay than that." A woman came and took their drink orders, two brandies.

"Changes? We don't hear much of Bruuch on Macrobastia, where I've been teaching. Some changes are obvious—" with an economical gesture he indicated their surroundings—"this port was only packed earth and a metal hut when I left last time. But I'm more interested in the Bruuchians than you colonists. Are things much the same with them?"

"Um . . . not really." Their brandies came; Crowell inhaled the fumes deeply and drank with obvious relish.

"No brandy in the Confederación like Bruuchian. A pity you don't export."

"The Company's supposed to be working on that. That and the native handcrafts." His shoulders twitched in a shrug. "But kilogram for kilogram, they make much more on rare earths. Every planet makes beverages and most have busy autochthones."

"Yes, the Bruuchians . . . things have changed?"

Jonathon took a small sip of brandy and nodded. "Both in the long view and, well, recently. Have you heard that the natives' average life-span is down?"

Otto McGavin knew but Crowell shook his head, no.

"In the past six years, down some twenty-five per cent. I think the average life-span of a male is down to about twelve years. Bruuchian, that is; about sixteen Standard. Of course, they don't seem to mind."

"Of course not," Crowell mused. "They would see it as a blessing." The Bruuchians preserved their dead in a secret rite and the carcasses were treated as living creatures, with more status in the family than anyone who was still moving around. They were consulted as oracles, the oldest living family member divining their advice by studying the corpses' immobile features.

"Any theories?"

"Well, most of the males work in the mines; there is some bismuth associated with the rare-earth deposits; bismuth is a powerful cumulative poison to their systems. But the mineralogists swear there's not enough bismuth in the dust they breathe to cause any health problems. And of course the creatures won't let us have a body for autopsy. It's a sticky situation."

"Quite so, I can see. But I recall the Bruuchians having enjoyed small doses of bismuth as a narcotic—could they simply have found a large source and gone on a species-wide orgy?"

"I don't think so. I've looked into the matter rather closely—God knows, Deirdre's always harping on it. There aren't any natural concentrations of bismuth on the planet, and even if there were, the creatures lack the technology, the basic grasp of science, needed to refine it." Crowell winced inwardly every time Lyndham called them "creatures."

"The Company doesn't mine it," Lyndham continued, "and it's on the 'forbidden imports' list. No, I really think bismuth poisoning is the wrong tack."

Crowell drummed two fingers on the table, gathering his thoughts. "Excepting metabolic quirks like that, they seem quite a hardy people. Could it be overwork?"

"No possibility, absolutely none. Ever since your book came out, there's been a Confederación observer, a xenobiologist, keeping track of the creatures. Every one that works in the mines has a serial number tattooed on his foot. They're logged in and out, and not allowed to spend more than eight hours a day in the mines. Otherwise, they would, of course. Strange creatures."

"True." In the home, Bruuchians were placid, even lazy. In places defined as work areas, though, they would routinely work themselves to exhaustion—not

31

exactly a survival trait. "Took me nine years to find out why." *The disappearances,* the Otto part of his brain was whispering, reminding . . . "You said something about 'recent' changes?"

"Um." Jonathon fluttered his hands and took another sip. "It's rather distressing. You know, we still have only about five hundred people on the planet, permanent personnel."

"Really? I'd expected more by now."

"Company doesn't encourage immigration; no jobs. At any rate, we're a pretty closely knit group; everybody knows just about everybody else. More like a family, we like to think, than just a group of people with a common employer.

"Well, people have been . . . missing, disappearing, over the past few months. They must be dead, since humans can't survive on native food, and our own food supply is closely monitored, all meals accounted for.

"All of them disappeared without a trace. Three people, to date, one of them the Supervisor of Mines. Quite frankly, the general consensus of opinion is that the creatures did them in for some—"

"Incredible!"

". . . and as you can imagine, a good deal of bad feeling has been generated. Uh, several of the creatures have been killed."

"But—" Crowell's heart was beating dangerously fast. He forced himself to sit back, take a deep breath, speak calmly: "There is absolutely no way a Bruuchian can take a human life. They don't have the concept of killing, not even for food. And as much as they revere their dead, and aspire to be a 'still one,' they never hurry the process . . . they can't grasp the idea of murder, or suicide, or even euthanasia. They don't even have *words* for these things."

"I know, but—"

"Do you remember that time, it was 218, I think, when a drunken worker killed a Bruuchian in the mines?

32

With a shovel; the native had backed a cart over the man's foot.

"I had to go to the village and find the proper household, try to explain. But the news got there before I did, and the household was in a delirious state of celebration—never had so young a one passed into stillness. They regarded it as a special favor from the gods. Their only concern was to recover the body and preserve it, and two of them were out on that chore when I arrived.

"When I told them that a man had done it, they thought I was jesting. Men are close to godhood, they said, but men are not gods. I tried to explain it over and over, using different . . . modes of address—but they only laughed. Finally they called in the neighbors and had me keep repeating the story for their amusement. They regarded it as a wonderfully blasphemous joke, and it was told and retold for years."

Crowell emptied his glass in one gulp.

"I can't say I disagree with you—the accusation is absurd. But they are powerful creatures, and a lot of people are growing afraid of them," Lyndham said. "Besides, the alternative explanation is that there's a murderer in our midst, in our family."

"Maybe not," Crowell said. "Maybe there's something in the planet's environment that we've overlooked before, some hidden danger. Did they drag the dustpits for bodies?"

"Some. Didn't find anything."

They talked for a half hour on this and less bizarre topics, but Crowell/McGavin learned nothing that hadn't already been programmed into him during four weeks of personality overlay. Lyndham was paged over the public-address system.

He got up to go. "Can I detail someone to get you to Transients, Isaac? I may be tied up for a while, cataloguing."

"No, I can find my way. You're still in import/export, then?"

33

"Yes, indeed. At the very top, now." He smiled. "Chief of the Imports Section. Which makes me very busy once a week, sorting through everything that comes in."

"Well, congratulations," Crowell said. McGavin moved the man up one notch on his list of suspects.

3

The two-wheeled cart lurched to a stop and Crowell got out carefully, heavily. He gave a small coin of Company money to the native who had pulled him over a kilometer, and said in the formal mode:

"For your labors / this small token."

The native took it in a huge trifurcate hand and placed the coin in his mouth, then tongued it to the voluminous pouch under his chin. He mumbled a ritual answer in the same mode, then scooped up Crowell's baggage and carried it through the open door marked TRANSIENTS' BILLET #1.

Crowell lumbered his large frame down the walk, envying the native's easy jog. The Bruuchian had a coat of short brown fur, now slightly misted with sweat. From the rear, he resembled a large Terran monkey, though he was tailless. His great splayed feeet were larger versions of the hands, with three mutually opposable toes. His legs were short in proportion to his body, with high knee joints that allowed movement some forty-five degrees from the perpendicular—in both directions. Thus his gait had a cartoonish character, amplified by the fact that his arms dropped straight from outsize shoulders to within a few centimeters of the ground.

There was nothing comic about his frontal aspect, though, with the two huge glaring eyes that never blinked (though a transparent nictitating membrane slid up and back every few seconds), and the forehead cluster of low-definition eyespots that, being sensitive to infrared, allowed him to find his way in almost total darkness. A huge mouth was covered by a single lip-flap, which curled up frequently to reveal a set of improbably large molars. He had ears that would resemble a cocker spaniel's, except that they were hairless and heavily veined.

This particular individual sported two concessions to his human employers: a pair of striking earrings and a loincloth concealing nothing of any conceivable interest to a human being. He also spoke two human words, "yes" and "no." That was about average.

The native was out the door again before Crowell had labored halfway there. He ran around Crowell without a word, harnessed himself to his cart, and rushed off.

Crowell went into his billet and sank onto the spartan bunk. He had lived in more elegant surroundings. The room had a crude table and chair of native manufacture, an unimaginative print of a winter scene on Terra, a military-type locker, and a shower operated by hoisting a perforated bucket to head level. There was another bucket to transport water in, a washbasin, and a fogged mirror. There being no other sanitary facilities, Crowell assumed they still had the outhouse he'd grown to hate ten years before.

He was debating whether to recline on the bunk (not sure he could get back up) when someone tapped on the door. "Come in," he said wearily.

A gangly young man with a wisp of beard stepped diffidently to just inside the door. He was wearing khaki shorts and shirt and carried two bottles of beer. "I'm Waldo Struckheimer," he said, as if that explained something.

"Welcome." Crowell couldn't take his eyes off the beer. It had been a dusty ride.

"I thought you might appreciate something to drink,"

he said, loping across the room in two steps, carefully uncorking a beer.

"Please . . ." Crowell gestured in the direction of the native chair and took a large swallow while Waldo was folding himself into a sitting position. "Are you also a transient?"

"Me? Oh, no." Waldo uncorked the other bottle, put both corks in his jacket pocket and thumbed it shut. "I'm the xenobiologist in charge of native welfare. And I hear you're Dr. Isaac Crowell. It's a pleasure to finally meet you."

They made polite noises for a minute. "Dr. Struckheimer, I've only talked to one other person since I landed . . . what he said was pretty alarming."

"About the disappearances?"

"That, too. But mainly the rapid decline in Bruuchian life-expectancy."

"You didn't know about that?"

"No, nothing."

Waldo shook his head. "I wrote an article for *J. Ex.* two years ago. Still hasn't come out."

"Well, you know how that goes. If it's not about Ember or Christy's World—"

"Bottom of the stack, yeah. No news like new news. Who did you talk to?"

"Jonathon Lyndham. He mentioned bismuth."

Waldo made a tent out of his long fingers and looked inside. "Well, that was the first thing I thought of. They do show most of the clinical signs, but they're common ones—like nausea or shortness of breath in humans. Anything from a hangover to cancer.

"I'd still favor bismuth—or something similar, like antimony—if there was any way in hell they could get it. Ever since we learned how toxic and addictive it was, nobody's been allowed to bring it onto the planet. Not even me, and I could use a few grams of the subgallate."

"Any way they could be getting it from the mines?"

36

"No. All the bismuth in ten cubic meters of that lanthanide ore wouldn't be enough to give a Bruucchian a slight buzz. I've come to think it's just a red herring. Something else is causing the symptoms."

"Any recent change in, well, their dietary habits, for instance? Human food?"

"No, they still live off the reptimammals; won't even look at human food. I've run a continuing analysis on the flesh-pods they harvest. Nothing unusual. No bismuth, certainly."

They sat for a moment in thoughtful silence. "Looks like this may be a bigger job than I'd anticipated. They sent me here, my publisher, to update the book for a new edition. I expected only to gather some new statistics and renew old friendships." He knuckled both eyes. "Quite frankly, the prospect of footwork is appalling. I'm not a young man any more, and I weigh twenty kilos more than I did last time. Even then, I needed Gravitol to get around comfortably."

"You don't have any yet?"

"No, haven't got around to it. Is Willy Norman still the Company doctor?"

"Yeah. Here." He unstuck a pocket and brought out a small vial. "Have a couple; I get them free."

"Many thanks." Crowell put two tablets on his tongue and washed them down with beer. A feeling of lightness and well-being pulsed through him. "Ah! Potent stuff." He stood without difficulty for the first time since he had become Isaac Crowell. "Could I impose on you for a tour of your lab? Seems like a logical starting place."

"Sure, I was going to stop by this afternoon anyway." A jinrikisha rumbled by outside. "Maybe we can catch that one." He went to the door and gave a piercing whistle.

The driver heard him and came to a halt in a shower of dust. He wheeled the cart around and rushed toward them as if his life depended on it. As they got on, he grunted one syllable: "Where?"

"Take-us-to-Mine-A-please." The Bruuchian gave a disarmingly human nod and pulled away with a powerful surge.

Mine A was three kilometers away. The ride was dusty and not too terrifying.

The lab was a large silver dome beside the mine elevator. "Nice setup," Crowell said as he beat dust from his clothes. "Dustpits?" The area between the road and the dome was clustered with roped-off circles.

"Yeah. No big ones."

Most dustpits were a meter or less deep—but step into a big one and you were gone forever. The natives could see dustpits plainly, night or day, since their infrared eyeclusters were sensitive to the temperature differential between the pits and the ground. But to human eyes, everything was uniform: smooth brown talc.

Nearing the lab, Crowell heard the chugging of an air compressor. The dome wasn't metal after all, but aluminized plastic, kept rigid by air pressure. They went through a flap door in the side.

The air inside was sweet and cool. "Compressor pushes cold air through a humidifier and a stack of dust filters. The Company gets a lot of free overtime for their investment."

The lab was an interesting combination of rustic and ultramodern. Every piece of furniture was the familiar Bruuchian design, but Crowell recognized the crinkly gray box of an expensive general-purpose computer, a caloric oven, a large-screen electron microscope, and a lot of complicated glassware that had to have been imported. There were several arcane devices that he couldn't identify.

"Impressive. How did you ever get the Company to finance all of this?"

Struckheimer shook his head. "They just paid for the

building—hard enough to get that! The rest is a Confederación grant from the Public Health Commission.

"So I'm the Company's veterinarian for six hours a day, and the rest of the time I do research on Bruuchian physiology. Or try to—it's difficult, without cadavers and exploratory operations."

"You can do X rays, though; neutron scans—"

"Sure I can." He pulled on his sparse beard and glowered at the center of Crowell's chest. "For whatever good it does. What do you know about Bruuchian anatomy?"

"Well . . ." Crowell hiked himself up onto a stool, which creaked. "The early studies were inconclusive, and I haven't—"

"Inconclusive! I don't know much more than that myself. They have several internal organs that seem not to have any function. Not all of them even have the same set of organs. And if they do, they aren't necessarily in the same place in the body cavity.

"The only consistent results I get are from that thing." He stabbed a thumb in the direction of a large structure that looked like a nineteenth-century diving bell. "Stokes chamber, for quantitative metabolic analysis. I hire them to sit in there and eat and excrete. They think it's a big joke."

He punched his palm with his fist. "If only I could get a cadaver! Did you hear about last month, the laser?"

"No, nothing."

"They say it was an accident; I have my doubts. Anyhow, a native fell, or was pushed, in front of a mining laser. Sliced him in two."

"God!"

"I was right up here; took me less than ten minutes to get down to where it happened. But relatives had already spirited the body away. Must have gone on one elevator while I was going down on the other. I took an interpreter and got to the village as fast as I could. Found his hut.

"I—I told them I could sew him back together again, I could cure him. God, I wanted to get a look at that body!"

He kneaded his forehead with two fingers. "They believed me. And they apologized. But they said they had thought he was ready for stillness, and they had already 'sent' him.

"I asked if I could see his body and they said, sure, they were happy that I would want to join the celebration."

"Surprised they'd let you," Crowell said.

"They've eased up on that. Anyhow, you know that room, the family room, where they keep their ancestors' mummies. I went in there; must have been fifty of them leaning against the walls, three and four deep, perfectly preserved.

"They pointed out the new arrival: he looked just like all the others, except for a hairless circle around his middle, where the laser had cut through. I looked at the ring of skin closely—they let me use a flashlight—and there was absolutely no seam, no scar! I checked the serial number on the foot, and it was the right one.

"The cadaver couldn't have gotten there ten minutes before I did . . . that kind of scar suppression takes induced skin regeneration, weeks of convalescence, and you can't do it on a dead organism.

"But try to find out how they do it—you might as well ask a person how he keeps his heart beating. I don't think they really understand the question."

Crowell nodded. "When I wrote my book, I had to be satisfied with a simple description of the phenomenon. All I could find out was that it involves some ritual using the oldest and youngest family members. And nobody teaches them what to do. They say it's obvious. But they can't explain, and they won't let you watch."

Struckheimer went to a big free-standing refrigerator

and got two beers. "Stand another one?" Crowell nodded and Struckheimer uncorked both of them. "Make it myself—one of the native boys tends the brew for me. Going to lose him in a few months, though —he's almost old enough for the mines."

He handed Crowell a beer and sat down on a lower stool. "I suppose you know they don't have anything like a study of medicine. No shamans or anything. If somebody gets sick, they just sit around and cheer him on, and if he recovers they offer him their condolences."

"I know," said Crowell. "How do you ever get them to come around for treatment . . . and, for that matter, how can you know what to do for them when they come in?"

"Well, my medical assistants—I've got four—inspect each of them when they go into the mine, and again after they've finished work. The Public Health Commission designed a remote diagnostic machine similar to the one a doctor uses. There are four of them all synched into my computer over there. It checks out their respiration rate, skin temperature, pulse, and such; if there's any significant difference between two consecutive readings, they send the fellow over to me. By the time he gets here, the computer has filled me in on his medical history, and I can dope out some empirical remedy based on clinical experience and physiological experiments. I never have any idea whether the remedy is going to reduce the symptoms. A drug will work perfectly on one of them, and on the next the symptoms will just get worse and worse until he curls up and dies. And you know what they say about that."

"Yeah—'He was ready for stillness.' "

"Right—they tolerate the treatment only because it's a condition for employment. They'd never come on their own."

"Have the diagnostic machines given you any clue as to the reason they're dying off so much younger than before?"

41

"Oh, sure . . . symptoms, in a statistical sense. For instance, the average respiration rate has increased more than ten per cent since we started taking readings. Average body temperature, up almost a degree. That supplements my clinical data; both together led to the original conclusion that it was cumulative poisoning. Bismuth would fit the data nicely, since I found in radioactive organ traces that it all accumulates in one organ and is never excreted.

"And it has to be something associated with the mines. You know, they keep careful demographic records; the families with the greatest number of recent additions to stillness have the most 'political' power. It turns out that the life expectancy of those who don't work in the mines hasn't changed a bit."

"I didn't know that!"

"The Company doesn't like it spread around."

They talked for another hour, Crowell mostly listening, Otto developing a plan.

4

It was almost dark when Crowell trudged up the walk to the doctor's office. The Gravitol had worn off and he was feeling miserable again.

The doctor's office had the first modern furniture, a conservative chrome-and-plastic desk, and the first attractive woman Crowell had seen on the planet.

"Do you have an appointment, sir?"

"Uh, no, ma'am. But I'm an old friend of the doctor's . . ."

"Isaac—Isaac Crowell! Come on back and say hello!" The voice came from a little intercom on her desk.

"Last room down the corridor to your right, Mr. Crowell."

Dr. Norman met him in the corridor and steered him

to a different room, pumping his hand. "It's been so long, Isaac—I heard you were back and frankly, I was surprised. This is no planet for oldsters like us." The doctor was an affable giant; red-faced and white-haired. They went into his living quarters, a two-room apartment with a worn carpet and lots of old-fashioned books on the walls. When they entered, music started playing automatically; Crowell couldn't identify it, but Otto knew: "Vivaldi," he said without thinking.

The doctor looked surprised. "Finally getting an education in your old age, Isaac? I remember when you thought Bach was just a kind of beer."

"I'm finding time for a lot of things now, Willy." Crowell lowered his bulk into an overstuffed chair. "All of them sedentary."

The doctor chuckled and strode into the kitchenette. He put ice in two glasses, measured brandy into each, and splashed soda into one, water into the other.

He handed the brandy and soda to Crowell. "Always remember a patient's prescription," he said.

"As a matter of fact, that's one thing I dropped by for." Crowell took a sip from his drink. "I need a month's supply of Gravitol."

The smile went off the doctor's face and he sat down on the couch, putting his drink down without sampling it. "No, you don't Isaac. A week's supply would be plenty. Then you'd be stone . . . cold . . . dead."

"What?"

"Obesity is a contraindication; at any rate, I never advise it for people over fifty-five. I never take it myself anymore. It would put too much of a strain on the old ticker."

My heart is thirty-two years old, McGavin thought, *and it's carrying around an extra fifty kilos. Think, think!*

"Is there some less potent drug that'd help me get around in this gravity? I've got a lot of work to do."

"Hmm . . . yes, Pandroxin isn't nearly as dangerous,

43

but it should give you a measure of comfort." He reached into a drawer and brought out a prescription pad. He scribbled a short note. "Here you go. But stay away from that Gravitol. It would be pure poison to your system."

"Thanks. I'll get it filled tomorrow."

"Tonight, if you want. The pharmacy part of the Company store's open all night now.

"So . . . what brings you back to this outlandish place, Isaac? Investigating the change in the Bruuchian death rate?"

"Not really, or not primarily. I just came to update my book for a new edition. But that *is* one of the things I'll want to look into. What do you think of the bismuth theory?"

Willy waved a hand in the air. "Hogwash. I think it's overwork, pure and simple. The little bastards work hard all day in the mines; then they go home and knock themselves out carving on that tough wood. You don't have to look any farther than that."

"They always have seemed hell-bent on working themselves to death. The males, anyhow. Somehow that seems too pat, though—the ones who don't work in the mines are always charging around, too. But they aren't popping off early."

The doctor snorted. "Isaac, go down tomorrow and watch them work the mines. It's a wonder they even last a week down there. The others look lazy compared to the mine workers."

"I'll do that." How to get the conversation around to the disappearances? "How about the human side of the colony? Changed much since I left?"

"Not really. Most of us got weaseled into twelve-or twenty-year contracts; same people around, only ten years older. Costs a year's salary to get back to Terra, and you forfeit that one-hundred-percent retirement if you break your contract—so most of us are sticking it out. Had four people buy their way out; I don't think you knew any of them.

"There's a new Confederación ambassador—like the three before him, nothing for him to do here. But the law says we've got to have one—I understand the Diplomatic Corps considers this the least of all possible worlds; being assigned here is either proof of incompetence or punishment for something. It's punishment for this one, Stu Fitz-Jones; he had the misfortune of being ambassador to Lamarr's World when the civil war broke out there. Not his fault, of course, it's just that nobody understood the natives' internal politics. But they had to hang it on somebody, so here he is. You ought to drop by and talk to him, he's an interesting fellow. But go in the morning while he's still a little bit sober.

"We've had six births, half of them legitimate, and eighteen deaths." Willy frowned. "Rather, fifteen deaths and three disappearances. All the disappearances in the past year. People have been getting careless. Outside the Company city, you might as well be on another planet. But people go out walking alone; prospecting or just getting away from the rest of us. They break a leg or step in a dustpit and it's all over. Two of the disappearances were brand-new people, probably Confederación agents"—Otto jumped, that was true—"and the other was old Malatesta, the Supervisor of Mines. I think that's what brought the two agents. They were supposed to be doing mineralogical research, but they didn't work for the Company. Who could have paid their way? Nobody else can mine on this planet."

"Could be a university paying for abstract knowledge—that's how I came here the first time."

The doctor nodded. "Exactly. That's what they claimed. But they weren't scholars, I could tell; I've lived and worked with academic people most of my life.

"Oh, they could identify themselves, and they seemed to know their subjects adequately, but . . . you know

45

that zombie thing the Confederación is supposed to use with its agents?"

"Vaguely—isn't it just plastic surgery and hypno-learning?"

"Oh, I suppose. Anyhow, that's what I think these fellows were; a couple of agents they'd made to walk, talk, and act like geologists. But they went to all the wrong places; like the mines—they've been analyzed and the analyses published down to the last molecule. And they never stuck to one place long enough to get any serious work done."

"You're probably right."

"You think so? Have another drink. Everybody else around here thinks I'm getting paranoid in my old age."

"Maybe we're both falling apart together." Isaac smiled. "Thanks for the offer, but I'd better pick up the Pandroxin and be getting back to my place before I collapse. It's been a long day."

"I can imagine. Well, good to see you again, Isaac. Still play chess?"

"Better than ever." Especially with Otto's help.

"Well, drop by some evening and we'll go a round or two."

"I'll do that. Take care."

5

Isaac didn't go to the pharmacy right away. He went to his billet and made a radiophone call.

"Biological lab. Struckheimer here."

"Waldo, this is Isaac Crowell. Could I ask a favor?"

"Fire away."

"I'm going down to Dr. Norman's office now, to get some Gravitol. Those tablets you gave me today seemed just about right—could you look up the dosage?"

"Don't have to look it up, it's five milligrams. But

look, Isaac, he'll probably want you on a smaller dose—the older you get, the less they give you."

"Really? Well, I'll try to talk him out of it. Seems to me it should go the other way around!"

"You'll never talk Willy out of anything. He's the most stubborn creature I've ever argued with."

"I know; we were good friends. Maybe he'll have pity on a fellow geriatrics-ward case."

"Well, good luck. See you again soon?"

"I'll be down your way tomorrow, checking out the mines."

"Stop in for a beer."

"Glad to." They rang off.

Crowell emptied his suitcase and flipped up the false bottom. He selected a stylus that was an ordinary ball-feed pen on one side and an ultrasonic ink eradicator on the other. Luckily, the doctor had used a black ball-feed to write the prescription; he wouldn't have to forge the signature.

He practiced writing "5 mg. Gravitol, quant suff 30 days" a couple of dozen times, then buzzed the Pandroxin prescription into invisibility and scrawled the counterfeit one over the signature.

The Company store was dark except for one light over the prescription desk. The front door was locked and Crowell dragged himself over to a side door. It slid open when he put his foot on the treadle-mat, and a bell rang.

A clerk came from behind the shelves of reagents, rubbing sleep from his eyes. "Something I can do for you?"

"Yes, I'd like this filled, please."

"Sure thing." The young man took it and walked back behind the shelves. "Say," he yelled back, "this isn't for you, is it?"

All Otto now. "Of course not. I use Pandroxin. That's for Dr. Struckheimer."

The clerk came back in a minute with a little green

47

vial. "I could have sworn Waldo was in here for Gravitol just last week. Maybe I ought to call up Dr. Norman."

"I don't think these are for his own use," Crowell said slowly. "They're for some experiment on the natives."

"Okay. I'll just put it on his account, then."

"That's funny. He gave me cash to pick them up."

The clerk looked at him. "How much?"

"Eighteen and a half credits."

Crowell extracted his wallet and counted out nineteen credits. Then he laid out a pink Cr50 bill next to it.

The clerk hesitated, then picked up the Cr50, folded it, and put it in his pocket. "It's your funeral, old-timer," he said as he rang up the purchase. "That's a young man's dosage."

Crowell took the half-credit change and left without a word.

6

The next morning, feeling human again, Crowell went out to the mines just after sunup. He checked at the dome, but Waldo wasn't there, so he ambled on down to Mine A.

A long line of Bruuchians at the entrance to the mine danced and waved their arms as if they were trying to keep warm. Their animated conversation got louder and louder as he approached the front of the line.

A human in white coveralls was examining the lead Bruuchian. He didn't notice Crowell until he was standing right next to him. "Hello there!" Crowell shouted over the din.

The man looked up, startled. "Who the hell are you?"

"Name's Crowell—Isaac Crowell."

"Oh, yeah—I was just a kid last time you were here. Watch this." He picked up a megaphone and shouted in Bruuchian (informal mode): "Your spirit/ disrupts my spirit/ slowing the progress/ of this line and your way to stillness." The conversation quieted to a low murmur. "See, I read your book." He continued making passes over the Bruuchian's body with a gleaming metal probe.

"Is that the diagnostic machine?" Crowell indicated a featureless black box clipped to the man's belt, with a cable leading to the probe.

"Yeah. It figures out whether anything's wrong with the beastie and tells Dr. Struckheimer." He clapped the Bruuchian on the shoulder: the "beastie" ran off into the mine. The next stepped up and presented his foot, his knee bending in an unkneelike manner. "It's also a microphone," he said, peering at the number tattooed on the Bruuchian's foot. He read the number off in slow, clear tones and began running the probe over the brown fur in a regular pattern.

"Ne can figure anybody gettin' off this planet, wantin' to come back. How much they have to pay you?"

"Well, there's a new printing of my book coming out. The publisher wants it updated."

The man shrugged. "Long as you got a ticket back, guess it's not so bad.

"If you wanta take a look downstairs, go ahead. But watch your step . . . they run around like crazy down there—keep away from the elevator and they probably won't trample you."

"Thanks." Crowell walked down the corridor to a small open elevator. Inside, one Bruuchian was doing an impatient little dance. Over the elevator, a sign said TWO AT A TIME. Bruuchians had no written language, but this one must have known the rule; as soon as Crowell had strapped himself in, the native pushed a big red button and the elevator fell abruptly. Crowell hung on while Otto counted dispassionately. Twenty-two seconds passed before the repulsors cut on and the machine squeezed to a halt. Even allowing for air resistance, they must be over a kilometer deep.

It was very dark, but then the Bruuchians didn't need as much light as Terrans. He could hear activity all around as the Bruuchians shouldered past him, but he couldn't see anything.

"Ah, Isaac," said a human voice three or four meters away. "You should have warned me that you were coming." A flashlight snapped on and the light bobbed up to Crowell.

"Here, put these on." He handed Crowell a pair of goggles. Nightglasses: the interior of the mine suddenly appeared, a ghostly green and gray video image.

"Things have certainly changed," Crowell said. "Why is it so dark?"

"They asked for it, said the light slowed them down."

"Good Lord." Crowell stared at the flurry of activity. "Makes me tired, just watching them." The mine was a roughly square cavern the size of a large hall. Some fifty Bruuchians, working in pairs, hacked away at three walls with vibropick and shovel. There was a barrow serving each pair of teams; as soon as the barrow was full, the Bruuchian who had been fidgeting beside it would zoom off to the fourth wall, where Crowell and Struckheimer stood, and dump the ore onto a conveyor that took it to the surface. Then he'd return and pick up a shovel; the former shoveler would get a vibropick; the pickmeister would fidget beside the barrow.

In the midst of all this activity, a small Bruuchian scurried back and forth scattering what appeared to be a mixture of sand and sawdust on the damp cave floor, narrowly escaping collision every few seconds. There was a zany order to it, like children knocking themselves out in a complicated relay race.

"You know," Crowell said, "Willy Norman thinks the decline in life expectancy is due to simple overwork. Looking at this, I'm inclined to agree with him."

"Well, they do work harder at this than at anything

else I've seen them do. Especially since we turned out the lights. But I'm allowed to adjust their work hours to compensate for the increased activity—how long a workday did they have when you were studying them?"

"Eleven, twelve hours, I guess."

"It's down to six and a half."

"Really? You have that much power over the Company?"

"In theory, yes; they should jump when I say 'rabbit.' Since their contract here is at the sufferance of the Confederación Public Health Commission, and I'm the only PHC representative. But I don't overdo it. I have to depend on them for manpower, supplies, utilities, mail. It's a pretty cordial relationship—but they know that there are five or six other concerns ready to snap up the contract if they make a mistake. So they're pretty good in their treatment of the natives.

"Besides, they haven't lost anything in terms of overall productivity. They can only run one mine at a time; they have two shifts now, with no overlap, and the mine is actually open longer. Total yield is more than it's ever been."

"Interesting." Welcome to the suspect list, Waldo. "So they're actually working *less* than they did when their life expectancy was higher?"

Waldo laughed. "I know what you're thinking. No, it can't be a case of atrophic degeneration; that would show up in the lab tests—besides, they work less in the mines now, but more in the village. You wouldn't recognize the place. Skyscrapers and—"

"Skyscrapers!"

"Well, that's what we call them—mud and straw buildings two, sometimes three stories high. It's another mystery . . . they have all the room in the world to expand their village radially. But somewhere they got the idea to go up instead of out. And it's quite a job; wattle and daub isn't supposed to take that kind of stress. Now, when they build a house, they have to

51

reinforce the whole thing with ironwood; it's almost a wooden building covered with a layer of mud. . . .

"Say—maybe *you* can find out why they're doing it. Nobody here's been able to get a straight answer out of them. But you can speak the dialect better than any of us. Besides, you're kind of a folk hero to them— even though I don't think any of them were alive last time you were here. They know you were responsible for a lot of the changes in their lives, and they're grateful."

It was damp and cold and Crowell shivered. "For bringing them closer to stillness," he said bluntly.

Waldo said nothing. There was a rumble and the elevator came to rest behind them. "Hi, boss; hi, Dr. Crowell. Well, I brought the beasties' meat. Want I should turn 'em off?"

Waldo looked at his watch. "Sure, go ahead." The assistant threw a switch mounted on the elevator housing and the vibropicks stopped singing. For a while there was a chorus of ragged chunk-sounds as the workers tried to keep going despite loss of power. Then, by ones and twos, they formed up a line at the elevator. The assistant gave each one a large meatfruit, which he would take back to his work area. The crews would each squat in a circle, munching and talking in low grunts.

"Well, we're not needed around here," said Waldo. "How would you like to take a look at the village?"

"Fine, fine. Just let me stop by the billet to pick up my notebook and camera."

"We'll go by the lab and get a couple of beers, too. It's hot upstairs."

7

The sun was blistering hot when the cart skidded to a stop outside the village, ending the breeze that had made the trip livable.

Crowell wiped the sweat and caked dust from his face and took a final swig of beer. "What'll we do with the empties?"

"Oh, just leave 'em in the cart. This is the fellow who tends the beer for me; he'll drop them off at the lab."

"God, it's hot." Crowell heaved his bulk to the ground.

Waldo squinted at the sun. "It'll be better in a couple of hours. I suggest we find some shade."

"Suits me." They went through the village gate and started walking down the path. They couldn't see anything but the grass, taller than a man, that surrounded the village in all directions for half a kilometer. Vehicles couldn't come in closer because of the skittish reptimammals that grazed here.

The beasts didn't seem to mind people walking through, though; Crowell and Struckheimer saw several of them, placidly gnawing grass, watching the humans with stalked eyes as they walked by. Most of them were over ten feet long, half of that length being unproductive tail and neck. But from their backs lolled strings of the meatfruit that formed the staple of the Bruuchian diet. Every female reptimammal (the males were set loose soon after birth and only let inside the compound for stud) supplied about thirty kilograms of meatfruit per season; every family had at least three or four of the creatures. Tending and harvesting the beasts was the major responsibility of the females.

The reptimammals were considered more than a source of meat, more than pets; they were actually low-status family members. They were "second-class citizens" because they couldn't speak and, more important, couldn't aspire to stillness—they just died. But the Bruuchians didn't eat the flesh of the dead reptimammals. They buried them with ceremony and mourning.

A native came loping down the trail toward them, moving much more slowly than the ones in the Company city did. He stopped in front of them and said in the informal mode:

"You are Crowell-who-jests and you are Struckheimer-who-slows./ I am young one called Baluurn/ sent to guide you on this visit."

His little speech over, the little Bruuchian fell in beside the two humans, trying to match step with Crowell.

"I know this one," Struckheimer said. "He's learned quite a bit of English. He's been my interpreter before."

"That's right," the creature belched in a strange burlesque of human speech. "All time in . . . creche I hear tapes you-Crowell leave."

This startled Crowell. He struggled with the informal mode: "The creche is for teaching/ the rituals of life and stillness./ Did you forego the teaching of your ancestors/ in learning to speak with humans?"

"The priest vouchsafed me/ my soul a special path to stillness/ and gave over my role as youngest/ to one of my brothers/ so that my time and mind could/ be used to plumb/ the ways and tongue of humans."

"What was that all about?"

"Well, he evidently had to use most of his learning year studying English—he said the priest gave him some sort of dispensation from learning the social rites. That usually takes most of their year."

"What word 'di-pensa-un' mean?"

"It's like 'permission,' Baluurn, but from a priest," Struckheimer said.

"That right. Priest give dipensa'un so I not-like brothers."

"Your English is very good, Baluurn. I studied your tongue for ten years and can't speak it as well as you speak mine."

Baluurn bounced his head in a nod. "Struckheimer-who-slows says human not-like Bruuchian. Learn more all long life but never so much one year. Must be for Bruuchian go into stillness much sooner than human."

The grass was thinning out and they could see the village ahead. Crowell immediately saw what Struckheimer meant—only about half of the dwellings were the familiar assymetric mud-and-wattle construction. The newer ones were all almost rectangular and up to ten meters high. "Baluurn, why did your people stop building the old way?"

He looked at the ground and seemed to be concentrating on not getting ahead of the humans. "It newkind . . . new part living ritual. Leave still ones near ground. Pass many time each day. Live above so pass still ones many time. Talk to still ones, still ones know more, still ones happier and more useful."

"I guess it makes sense," Waldo said with a straight face. "You couldn't expect them to know what was going on, locked up in a back room."

"Oh, never locked. Lock human word, no Bruuchian. But you right, still ones more useful."

Crowell fingered the small camera clipped to his belt. This could get in the way of one of his ideas. "I thought it was forbidden to move a still one; a new family had to be started if you moved one."

"That true, very true. New house built around old house. Take off old roof, leave hole in living house floor, buy rope Company store, pass by still ones climbing up and down many time every day."

"Quite so." Crowell took the camera from his belt and took some pictures of the buildings. Then he scribbled descriptions of each picture in his notebook. Protective coloration.

"For some reason they must want to have larger families," Waldo said. "I know they used to split the still ones and the family when it got too crowded and start a new family on the outskirts of the village."

A native woman walked by, leading two docile reptimammals. The fresh brown ooze on their backs showed they had just been pruned. Crowell snapped a picture.

"Larger families, maybe. But this building up instead of out also preserves grassland; that might be important." (Baluurn was silent through this exchange—he was used to humans going off in sudden *non sequiturs*. *He* knew why they were building up, just as he had told them. It was part of the living ritual now.)

"Crowell-who-jests?"

"Yes, Baluurn?"

"One family asked you visit. Old, very old woman remembers you. Would speak you before stillness, very soon."

"Say, that's odd . . . I asked them if anyone remembered you and they said all had passed into stillness."

Crowell smiled. "You used the formal mode, right?"

"Sure, who can handle the other?"

"Well, they probably misunderstood you, then. It's hard to talk about females in the formal mode, requires a certain amount of circumlocution. They thought you were asking if any *men* who remembered me were still alive."

"Crowell-who-jests right. Struckheimer-who-slows should sent for me talk. All village know old Shuurna."

"Well, let's go see her. Should be interesting."

Shuurna's building was one of the new high-rises. The two men and the Bruuchian filed in through the narrow door.

It was a claustrophobic room, filled from floor to ceiling with the old hut, with less than a meter of floor-space between the old door and the new one. It was dark and damp and smelled of mold.

Baluurn called out a ritual of entrance and someone upstairs responded. They entered the old hut and were surrounded by dozens of standing corpses, the family's still ones, whose open eyes regarded them without expression. Baluurn whispered something in the mode of piety, too fast for Crowell to follow, and said, "I go up first see Shuurna ready speak Crowell-who-jests."

Baluurn clambered quickly up the rope, looking more monkey-like than ever. "Hope it'll hold me," Crowell muttered, taking a Gravitol. He put the pillbox back and took something else from his pocket. Keeping an eye on the hole in the ceiling, he sidled over to one of the still ones resting against the wall.

"What are you doing, Isaac?"

"Just a second," Isaac whispered, reaching behind the still one. He returned and handed a small plastic envelope to Waldo. He put a small vibroknife back in his pocket. "A scraping from the shoulder," he whispered.

Waldo's eyes got round. "Do you know . . ."

Baluurn was sliding back down the rope. Two others followed him. "Shuurna wants speak Crowell-who-jests alone."

"Well, I'm game," he said. "If I can make it up that rope." Crowell got a good grip and heaved himself up, catching the slack end between his feet. With an extra Gravitol in him, it wasn't really hard, but he huffed and muttered and went up very slowly.

Shuurna was lying on a woven mat. She was the oldest Bruuchian Crowell had ever seen, hair yellowed and falling out in patches, eyes clouded with blindness, shrunken dugs loose gray flaps of flesh. She spoke the informal mode in a weak voice.

"Crowell-who-jests/ I knew you in my year of learning/ so I remember you better than my own children./ You walk differently now/ your steps seem a young man's steps."

"The years have been kinder to/ me than to you/ Shuurna who awaits stillness./ This apparent youth though/ is from an herb/ the doctor gave me to/ give me the strength of a younger man." This was something Crowell hadn't foreseen.

"My large-eyes are darkened/ but my many-eyes tell me/ that you are taller by two kernels/ Crowell-who-jests/ than you were my lifetime ago."

"This is so./ It is something that may/ happen to a human as he ages." You can add centimeters with plastiflesh, but you can't take them off.

There was a long silence that would have been considered awkward in human society.

"Shuurna/ do you have something to/ tell me or ask me?"

Another long pause. "No./ You who look like Crowell-who-jests/ I waited to see you/ but now you are not here./ I cannot wait longer/ I am ready for stillness./ Please summon the youngest and the new oldest."

Crowell walked to the rope. "Baluurn!"

"Yes, Crowell-who-jests."

"Shuurna is ready to . . . pass into stillness. Can you find the oldest and the youngest?"

The two who had come down with Baluurn scampered back up the rope. They walked by Crowell and stood before Shuurna. Crowell started to leave.

"Crowell-who-jests," the older one spoke, "/would you help us/ with our joyful burden?/ I am too old and this one is too small/ to carry Shuurna/ to join the other still ones downstairs."

Other still ones? Crowell went over to the three and stooped to take Shuurna's hand. It was solid, unyielding as wood.

"Old man in the family of Shuurna/ I do not understand./ I thought no humans could be present during/ the stillness ritual."

The old man nodded in that disarmingly human way. "This was so/ until not-long ago/ when the priests told us of the change./ To my poor knowledge/ you are only the second human/ to be so honored."

Crowell took up Shuurna's body unceremoniously, a hand under stiff arm and thigh. "To what other human/ befell this honor?"

The old one had his back to Crowell, following the youngster who was scampering to the rope. "I was not there/ but I was told/ it was Malatesta-the-highest."

Porfiry Malatesta, the last Supervisor of Mines, the first disappearance.

The rope threaded through an iron ring (also purchased at the Company store), and normally hung as a single strand, a stick tied to one end preventing it from slipping through the ring. Crowell balanced Shuurna's corpse on its feet and the old one passed the rope under her arms, securing it with something that was almost a square knot. They passed the body down to Baluurn, who untied it, and, balancing it with one hand, pulled in slack until the rope was in its original position. Then the two Bruuchians clambered down, hand over hand. Crowell followed with a little less confidence.

During the whole process, Waldo stood to one side, looking rather lost. The old one addressed Crowell in the informal mode, and Crowell replied with what Waldo recognized as a polite refusal. "Uh—what was that all about?"

"We were invited to the wake—you know, recite all the good deeds the old gal was responsible for and help decide where to lean the body. I told them no, thanks. These affairs last all day, and I've got an appointment. Besides, I've always gotten the feeling that having humans present puts a damper on the festivities. They have to invite you, of course, if you're anywhere nearby when the thing starts."

"And we're about as near as anybody's ever been. Glad you didn't accept for us—this whole business has gotten me a little qeuasy."

"Well, we can leave any time. Baluurn's staying, naturally."

"Let's go."

The sun was still blazing overhead when they stepped out of the hut. The whole experience couldn't have taken more than half an hour. They walked down the dusty road a few meters before Waldo spoke in a hoarse whisper.

"That sample you gave me . . . what makes you think they won't find out you took it?"

"Don't be so damned furtive! We're just tourists, right?

"You'd need a magnifying glass to find where I made the incision. Besides, I took it from one of the least accessible corpses, right up against a wall; with their taboo against moving them, we're safe."

"Well, I'll have to admit it is a windfall. Maybe we can finally figure out how—say, you were there when the woman died! Did you see anything?"

Crowell stared at the ground for a few steps before replying. "I was leaving, backing out; I was sure they didn't want me around. But they just went up to her and looked at her and said it was done. Whatever kind of embalming they do, they must do it while the person's still alive." Crowell shuddered in the heat. "They didn't even touch her."

8

Crowell had deliberately ignored Dr. Norman's advice, and had made an appointment with the ambassador in the early evening. He expected that the man would be pretty intoxicated by then. A strikingly handsome man—aristocratic features, gray hair flowing onto broad shoulders—answered the door.

"Ambassador Fitz-Jones?"

"Yes . . . oh, you must be Dr. Crowell. Come in, come in." He didn't seem too far gone.

Crowell walked into an elegantly appointed room, which the Otto part of his mind identified as being furnished in American Provincial, late twentieth century. Even if they were fakes, the shipping costs were staggering to contemplate.

Fitz-Jones indicated an amorphous leather-covered chair, and Crowell allowed it to swallow him. "Let me get you a drink. You may have brandy and water, brandy and soda, brandy and juice, brandy and ice, brandy and brandy, or—" he gave a conspiratorial wink —"a bit of Chateau de Rothschild burgundy, '23."

"Good God!" Even Crowell knew what that vintage represented.

"Somehow a small cask of it was mistakenly delivered here, instead of a case of badly needed immigration forms." He shook his head gravely. "These things are inevitable concarp—'scuse me—concomitants of trying to operate within the framework of an interstellar bureaucracy. We learn to adjust."

Crowell revised his earlier estimate. Fitz-Jones could well have been adjusting all day. "That sounds wonderful." He watched the man's careful steps and marveled at the human organism's ability to cope with proven toxins.

He came back with two highball glasses filled with the deep red wine. "No proper glassware, of course. Perhaps it's just as well. '23 doesn't travel well, you know—and it won't keep; have to drink it up quickly."

It tasted quite good to Crowell, but Otto could tell that it was rather bruised. Barbarous treatment for the wine of the century. Fitz-Jones took a delicate sip that somehow managed to deprive the tumbler of two centimeters of wine. "Did you have anything specific to see me about?—not that I don't enjoy company whenever it comes my way."

"Guess I just wanted to meet somebody else who wasn't working for the Company. I need an outsider's view of what's been happening the past ten years. Quite a bit, I understand."

Fitz-Jones made an expansive gesture that came within a millimeter of spilling wine. Otto could appreciate the years of practice that had gone into the perfection of that ploy. "Not really, not really . . . up until a year ago, of course. Until then it was just the workaday grind of running this, you'll excuse the expression, world.

Absolutely nothing for *me* to do while everybody else kept the sweatshop working. Submit a blank report twice a year.

"Then we had the disappearances, of course. Superintendent Malatesta was the official head, titular ruler, of this planet, so you can *imagine* the paperwork I went through. I was on the subspace radio for *hours* every day, until the . . . can you keep a secret, Dr. Crowell?"

"As well as the next man, I suppose."

"Well, it's not really a secret anymore, since the doctor—Dr. Norman, that is—figured it out. It's probably all around the Company by now. Anyhow, I talked to the Confederación officials on Terra, and they agreed to send a couple of investigators. Well, they came here—gave a splendid imitation of two scientific chaps—and while they were poking around, they disappeared, too."

"The two geologists?"

"Precisely. And you'd think that, with two of their men gone, the Confederación would send an army down here to see what's going on. But no. I finally talked to some undersecretary, and he told me they just couldn't afford any more men for our 'petty intrigues' on Bruuch."

"That's odd." The first item in the one report the agents had filed had been a warning about the untrustworthiness of the ambassador.

"Indeed. So I don't think the agents disappeared the way Malatesta did, you know, dead. They must have had a light cruiser hidden off somewhere, and when they found what they were after, they just left. Damned frustrating, you know; *we* still haven't the faintest idea of what happened to Malatesta. I'm certain that they found out."

It's quite likely they did find out, Otto thought. "Couldn't the Confederación have sent more agents without telling you?"

"No, impossible; violation of Confederación law. I'm the sole federal official on this planet. I must be notified.

And besides, only two people have come in since the agents disappeared. One was Dr. Struckheimer's new assistant; I've kept my eye on him. I think he must be just what he says he is; dull fellow, really. The other newcomer, of course, is you."

Crowell chuckled. "Well, I rather fancy being a spy. Will you ply me with wine frequently, then?"

Fitz-Jones smiled, but his eyes were cold. "Of course —as I said, it won't keep.

"Confidentially, I am rather expecting another agent to show up, whether they tell me about it or not. It could be anybody. You know that personality overlay technique—"

"The zombie business?" Crowell echoed Dr. Norman's words.

"Exactly. They can make a xerox copy of anybody. Anybody they can kidnap and hold for a month, anyhow." He drained the last of his wine. "This puts a distinguished, shall we say a 'well-exposed' person, such as yourself, above suspicion, of course. Too many people would notice your absense." And his eyes told Otto again: he's lying, he suspects.

The ambassador levered himself out of the oversized cushion. "Here, let me freshen your drink." He came back with two full glasses.

"Thanks. Oops, time to take my Pandroxin." He took a pillbox from his pocket and washed two pills down, one Gravitol and one alcohol suppressant.

"Ah, weak stuff, that. You must have a time here. Won't they let you take Gravitol?"

"No; I asked for it, naturally. But they say I'm too old and too fat." How dangerous is this subtle drunkard? "You have any theory about Malatesta?"

He shrugged and repeated the sloshing gesture. "I really don't know. I'm sure of one thing, though. This nonsense about the creatures being responsible is just that, a pile of snuurgsh—'scuse me—hogwash."

"I agree. They simply aren't capable of violence."

63

"Not only that. Malatesta was a great favorite of theirs. He even learned quite a bit of the language. They adopted him into one of the families, an honorary Bruuchian."

"I didn't know that."

"Oh yes, he went to a lot of their get-togethers. That priestly council made him an advisor of some sort."

"Yes," Crowell mused, "I heard today that he had been present at one of their stillness rituals."

"Where they embalm the poor creatures? Well, *I* didn't know that. Wonder why he didn't tell anybody about it? Struckheimer would've been his friend for life."

"Well, as you say, the Bruuchians couldn't have done away with Malatesta; so it must have been either an accident or murder. I guess the agents investigated both possibilities."

"Presumably. They seemed to spend most of their time dredging dustpits. Supposedly taking samples, actually looking for a body, I guess.

"I suppose the prime murder suspect would be Kindle, the new Supervisor. But he never wanted the job—it's twice as much work for only a pittance more pay. Besides, he's worried that whatever happened to Malatesta could happen to him too."

"You know him well, then?" Watch it, getting too inquisitive.

"Oh, quite well. He was in the Civil Service when I was posted on Lamarr's World. He had a considerable block of stock in the Company, and when the Assistant Supervisor position became open, he came out here and took the job. I was transferred here about a year later, and we just picked up where we had left off."

Time to change the subject. "Lamarr's World. I've heard of it, of course, but I've never been there."

"It was a lovely world." Fitz-Jones started the sloshing gesture but checked himself. "Especially compared to this desolation."

They talked of this and other harmless topics for

about an hour. Crowell stifled a yawn. "I really must be going. Excuse me for being a poor guest, but I tire so easily in this gravity."

"Oh, excuse *me* for being an inconsiderate host. I can be quite a bore, I know." Fitz-Jones helped Crowell up. "I'm afraid you may have some trouble getting a taxi at this hour."

"No, no problem. I can walk the few blocks." They exchanged amenities and Crowell lurched away convincingly.

9

His room had been searched by an amateur; Fitz-Jones' assistant, probably. He hadn't caught the hairs pasted over the closet door and suitcase lid, or even the pencil propped against the front door. Crowell sighed. Otto was worthy of more.

Anyhow, there was nothing incriminating in the billet itself. Crowell went outside to the outhouse, went in, and latched the door. Trying to ignore the smell, he took out a penstick and removed the cap. Doing so caused the pen to emit an invisible beam of ultraviolet light. Crowell shook the contact lens out of the cap and placed it in his left eye. With it, he could see quite well, though it would still be pitch black to light amplifiers or infrared eye clusters.

The hair across the loosened board was still in place. He lifted the board and removed the case that had been his suitcase's false bottom. He took a few items from it, replaced it, and smoothed the hair down in the position he had memorized.

At midnight the streetlights went off. Crowell donned the nightglasses he had bought at the Company store and walked the kilometer to the main warehouse without meeting anyone.

Knowing that any guard would also be equipped with

65

nightglasses, Crowell approached the building on a parallel street a block away and sat quietly behind the edge of a building for a half hour, watching the entrance.

Satisfied that the warehouse was unguarded, he crossed to the entrance and studied the lock. It was a simple magnetically coded padlock, and he opened it in a couple of minutes with a desensitizer and a set of picks.

When he closed the door behind him, the light level dropped below the nightglasses' threshold and Crowell had to use his ultraviolet penstick to see. It was made for close work, but he could get around with it. Directed at his feet it made a bright spot surrounded by a vague circle about a meter in diameter. He couldn't get any overall view of the warehouse, though, just a dim impression of crates stacked around.

He wasn't looking for anything specific, and really didn't have any great expectations. It was just another part of the routine, like going through the mines. He wished it had been possible to get around there without a guide, when it was empty.

Crowell walked around for an hour or so, examining every useless detail. At the other end of the warehouse he came to an open door. *Since it's open, h*e thought, *there can't be anything worth hiding inside.* But he went in to check.

There was a wide trough along one wall. It proved to be filled with a mixture of sand and sawdust, probably from the native ironwood. The opposite wall was stacked high with plastic bags filled with the same substance. At the end of the room were a sink and a couple of large buckets. A shelf above the sink held several cans the size of half-liter paint cans. Evidently this was the place where they prepared the substance that kept the natives from slipping on the wet mine floors.

He inspected the sink and it was just a dirty sink. The cans above had been inexpertly lettered ANTISEPTIC.

He picked one up and shook it; it was about three-quarters full of some powder. He flashed the light on the bottom and top, and on the top was a faint legend saying BISMUTH NITRATE CRYSTALS C.P. 1/2 KG.

Crowell almost dropped the can in surprise. Evidently the original label had been eradicated, but a trace of it was visible in ultraviolet. He replaced the can and sat back against the sink. This accounted for the natives' shortened life-span, and for the frantic activity in the mine; bismuth was a powerful stimulant and euphoric for them, as well as a cumulative poison. They must absorb it through their feet as they worked.

Now who would be responsible? The workers who mixed the bismuth nitrate into the sand-sawdust mixture probably didn't know what was going on; otherwise why not just leave the cans blank? Were the cans altered before they were shipped in? That seemed likely, since everybody seemed to know about the bismuth theory. Better have a talk with Jonathon Lyndham, new Chief of Imports.

Outside it was just as dark as it had been when Crowell had first broken into the warehouse. He snapped the padlock and gratefully stripped the thin plastic gloves off his hands.

There was an almost inaudible click behind Crowell and to his left. The Crowell-mind reacted even before the Otto-mind could think "safety switch," and Crowell rolled into a ditch on the side of the road. He was blinded as his nightglasses fell off, but looking up he could see a bright red pencil of light fan the road at waist level and flicker out. By then he had slid a miniature air pistol out of its pocket holster. He aimed at where the fading retinal afterimage showed the scarlet dot of a laser muzzle, and squeezed off four silent shots in rapid succession. He heard at least three of them ricochet from the warehouse wall, then the shuffle of a human running away.

Precious seconds finding the nightglasses, another second to sort out the images and see the man running, nearly a block away. Extreme range for this little popgun; Crowell aimed very high, fired and missed, fired and missed, and on the third try the man stumbled to the ground, but then staggered back to his feet and continued running, holding his arm. He still had the laser pistol in his hand, but didn't seem disposed to use it. Good thing, Otto thought; if the man were a professional he would have figured out how lightly armed Crowell was—and would have just flattened down at that extreme range and given Crowell a leisurely roasting.

He studied the rapidly dwindling figure. Nobody he recognized. Neither especially fat nor thin nor tall nor short. Crowell had to admit that he probably wouldn't know the man the next time he saw him. Unless he had that arm in a sling or cast, which wasn't unlikely.

As soon as Crowell stepped into his billet, the radiophone started buzzing. He stood beside it for several seconds; then, with a mental shrug, he picked up the transceiver.

"Crowell here."

"Isaac? Where have you been at this hour? This is Waldo—I've been trying to get you since three."

"Oh, I woke up and couldn't get back to sleep . . . so I took a little walk to tire myself out."

"Well, I . . . look, pardon me for calling so late, but . . . that sample you gave me—some of the cells in it are still alive!"

"Still alive? From a two-hundred-year-old mummy?"

"And undergoing mitosis—you know what mitosis is?"

"Cells dividing, yeah, chromosomes . . ."

"It was just a coincidence—I had the incubator stage on the microscope, that helped; I just put the sample in there rather than go through the rigmarole of changing to a regular stage. There was an interesting cell, a big nerve cell, that had evidently died in the middle of the anaphase—of mitosis, that is . . . I looked at it for a minute and then went off to get a beer, got sidetracked by some maintenance I had to do on the spectrometer—anyhow, I got back to the microscope a couple of hours later, and that same nerve cell was in a different part of the anaphase! Those cells are growing and dividing, but at a rate that must be several hundred times slower than normal Bruuchian cells."

"That's incredible!"

"It's more than incredible—it's impossible! I don't know, Isaac. I'm a generalist, just an overeducated veterinarian. We need a couple of real biologists—and we'll have them, too, dozens of them, as soon as the word gets out. Suspended animation, that's what it adds up to. Why, I wouldn't be surprised if those Bruuchians had a hundred people studying them a year from now."

"You're probably right." For the first time, Crowell wondered who might be listening in.

10

"Glad you could make it, Isaac." Dr. Norman's handshake was unusually firm.

"Couldn't pass up a chance to beat you again after all these years, Willy."

"Ha—believe I was four wins ahead when you left. Match you for white." Willy removed the tray with his dishes from the chess table.

"No, Willy, you go first. Out of consideration for your youth and inexperience."

The doctor laughed. "Pawn to King–4 and I'll fix you a drink."

Crowell pulled a chair over to the chessboard and set up the men, making Willy's first move for him. He looked at the pieces for a second and started his own opening game. "Have you talked to Waldo today?"

"Oh yes, the mummy thing. Quite fantastic. He was most secretive as to how he came upon a sample, though. I can just see Waldo skulking into one of those huts with his dissecting kit."

Dr. Norman set a drink down beside Crowell and took the chair opposite him. "I don't suppose *you* had anything to do with it, Isaac?"

"Well," Crowell said cautiously, "I'm pretty sure how he got the sample. But, as you say, it's a deep dark secret right now."

"This world is full of secrets." The doctor made his second move.

Crowell responded almost instinctively, a stock opening.

"A Ruy Lopez, Isaac? You're getting conservative in your old age. Your opening game used to be quite unpredictable."

"And you used to be four wins ahead."

The game went on for about an hour, with neither man saying much. Isaac was ahead in both position and strength when Dr. Norman looked up and said, "Who are you?"

"What did you say, Willy?"

The doctor took a piece of paper out of his pocket, unfolded it, and tossed it into the middle of the board. "If you were Isaac Crowell, you'd be dying or dead, on Gravitol. And don't tell me you aren't on it—Pandroxin gives a yellowish cast to the skin. You don't have it. Besides, your chess style is wrong: good, but all wrong. Isaac never knew how to play position."

Crowell finished off his drink, mostly melted ice, and leaned back in the chair. He stuck his right hand in his pocket and aimed the pistol under the table at the doctor's abdomen. "My name is Otto McGavin. I'm an agent for the Confederación. But please continue to call me Isaac—I'm more Crowell than McGavin in this persona."

The doctor nodded. "And you've done a very good job. Much more convincing than those other two—that is why you came here, isn't it, to investigate their disappearance?"

"Investigate their deaths. Every agent has a monitor implanted in his heart; they stopped broadcasting."

"Well, needless to say, your secret's safe with me."

"You shouldn't be burdened with it too much longer. I expect to have things out in the open within a day or two. Down to business, now—" Crowell moved a knight and said, "Mate in three."

"Yes, I saw that coming." Willy smiled. "I was hoping to distract you."

"Doctor, I think you missed your calling." Otto relaxed a little. "I was wondering how to ask you this without arousing suspicion . . . have you treated any gunshot wounds lately?"

"What! Why?"

"Somebody tried to ambush me last night, I shot him."

"My God . . . in the arm, was it?"

Crowell took out his pistol, opened the magazine, and let one of the small pellets roll onto the chessboard. "A wound in the right arm, this size projectile."

Dr. Norman rolled the pellet between his thumb and forefinger. "Yes, it was this small. The very devil to get out, too. And the wound was in the right arm." He took a deep breath. "Early this morning, Ambassador Fitz-Jones and Superintendent Kindle woke me up to take a pellet out of Kindle's arm. They said they had been up drinking and decided to try some target practice in the ambassador's back yard. Fitz-Jones had accidentally shot Kindle; he was most apologetic. They both reeked of wine, but acted quite sober. Kindle was in some pain; it looked as if they had tried to get the pellet out themselves. But it was too deep."

71

"Kindle—I've never met him."

"It seems you did meet him, last night. It's hard to believe. He seems such a meek fellow."

"You might as well know the whole story. If anything happens to me, try to get word to Confederación authorities.

"Some group of persons, including but not necessarily limited to the ambassador and the superintendent, is systematically poisoning the Bruuchians who work in the mines. The only motivation I can see is that it makes them work harder; increases profits.

"Say, Kindle owns a large part of the Company, doesn't he? I wonder whether Fitz-Jones also has an interest."

"I don't know," Dr. Norman said. "He claims to be independently wealthy. I can see that he might well be investing in the Company, though. Profits have quadrupled in the past few years. Why, I've been thinking of investing, myself, as a retirement income."

"Maybe you better not. Profits will be going down pretty soon."

"I suppose. Well, it is a horrible thing, even though I don't much care for the little boogers myself. What can I do to help?"

"I've got to use subspace radio. The only two on the planet are the superintendent's and the ambassador's. If you can get one of them here for an hour or so, I'll be able to call in the arrest and get authority to confine them."

"That'll be easy enough. Fitz-Jones and I have to fill out an accident report and take it to the Company clerk for witnessing. I told him to come by at around three this afternoon; it'll take more than an hour."

"You couldn't get Kindle to come up too, could you?"

"Afraid not. I've already confined him to quarters—wouldn't do to erode my authority in these matters by telling him to come over for a chat . . . but you're in no danger from him. I had to make a deep incision in his right triceps; he's going to be either doped up or in considerable pain for at least a week."

"Can't say that I have too much sympathy for him. Well, then, I'll pay a visit to the ambassadorial residence at about three o'clock. Here, take this." Crowell handed the pistol to Dr. Norman. "I'm afraid I've set you up as a secondary target."

Dr. Norman turned the little weapon over on his palm. "Won't you be needing this thing more than I?"

"No, I'm going to pick up some heavier artillery. Kindle had a laser pistol last night; if he'd known what he was doing, he could have fried me with no trouble."

"Well, I'll certainly keep it. But I've never fired a gun in my life."

"Well, be careful; that pistol doesn't have a safety. Just aim it in the right general direction and start pulling the trigger—it has over a hundred shots left in the magazine."

The doctor dropped it into the capacious front pocket of his lab coat. "I hope you get them safely incarcerated before I have to use it."

"They should be in the Company jail before dark tonight."

11

From his billet window Crowell could see the ambassador roll away toward the dispensary. He unplugged the laser pistol and checked the charge on it—more than half full, two minutes of continuous operation, which would be about enough to take on a platoon of infantrymen. He held both the pistol and his burglar's kit in his right hand, and draped a light jacket over them.

He set out walking down the street away from the ambassador's house, then circled around and came up behind the place. There were no buildings to obscure Fitz-Jones's view of the desert, which rolled in from the horizon to within a few meters of a large picture window.

Crowell took a crayon from his kit and inscribed a large black circle on the window. The black turned to chalky white and the circle of plastic fell out. With considerable effort he pulled himself up to the hole and through. He swallowed a Gravitol—only one more in his pillbox—and reflected on how good it would be to get his real body back again.

He checked three rooms before he found the radio, in the study. There was a cover over the sending plate and he cursed aloud when he saw that it had a thumbprint lock on it. It would take hours to open it.

Nothing for it but to wait until Fitz-Jones returned, and force him to open it. Crowell had an uncharacteristically macabre thought as he felt the weight of the vibroknife in his pocket. He only needed the man's thumb.

After wandering around Fitz-Jones's study for half an hour, learning nothing, Crowell remembered the Chateau de Rothschild. Might as well enjoy the wait. Crowell walked over the thick carpet to the kitchen. He found a glass, stuck the laser in his belt, and tapped the cask of wine.

"Don't do anything foolish, Isaac."

Otto turned slowly. *Mark II Westinghouse antique laser safety off right-hand range three meters set on full dispersion no chance.* "Why Jonathon. Fancy meeting you here." *Hand shaking but full dispersion can't miss hasn't fired yet probably won't thinkthinkthink . . .*

"I'm surprised at you, Isaac. Such language I heard you use. But you aren't really Isaac, are you? Any more than those other two were geologists. You'll be joining your friends tonight, Isaac. You can talk old times out in the dustpit."

"Shut up!" Another man came into view, his right arm stiff in a tractor cast. "Give me that gun." He took it in his left hand. Otto noted that he was trembling even more than the other, but it was pain, and probably anger, rather than nervousness. "Now go disarm him."

Kill him use body as shield would work one gee Otto-body but Crowell-body too slow too big . . . Jonathon plucked the gun from his belt and hopped back. "You aren't as dangerous as Stuart said you would be."

"He's dangerous, all right. But we've pulled his fangs. Go on back to your office, Lyndham. Fitz and I'll finish this job; you're the only one without any good reason for being here."

Jonathon went out the front door. "Well, Mr. McGavin—I suppose you find this rather embarrassing, to be held at bay by a 'meek fellow' like me.

"Yes, we heard your whole conversation this morning —Dr. Norman's radiophone really doesn't work too well, and neither does Dr. Struckheimer's; they broadcast all the time, straight into a recorder in my office." He motioned with the gun. "Come sit in the living room, Mr. McGavin. By all means bring your wine. I'd love to join you, but my good hand is full—that should make it even easier to kill you when the time comes."

Crowell sat in the old-fashioned chair and wondered when the time would come. "You can't actually think you can keep getting away with this."

"It's a big dustpit, the biggest. I'm afraid Doctors Norman and Struckheimer will be following you into it, too. We can't afford to have dozens of specialists prying around."

Crowell shook his head. "If I don't report, you're going to have to contend with more than a handful of scientists. A battle cruiser will land in your port and put the whole Goddamn planet under arrest."

"Strange they didn't do it when the first two agents disappeared. That's a pretty clumsy bluff, McGavin."

"Those two good men were agents, Mr. Kindle, but just agents. I'm a prime operator, one of twelve such.

75

You can ask Fitz-Jones what that means when he gets back."

"You may not be alive when he gets back. He didn't want to kill you here, because that would entail dragging your body over nearly a kilometer of desert. But it occurs to me that we could make more than one trip."

"A grisly alternative. Do you actually think you could cut up a man as if he were a side of beef? Very messy."

"I'm desperate . . ."

"Whatever are you two talking about?" Fitz-Jones came in through the hall entrance. "I saw Jonathon on the way here. I thought he was supposed to wait with you until I got back."

"I was afraid he'd do something stupid, so I told him to go on. Never did feel I could trust the man very much."

"You may be right. But I didn't want to leave you alone with this expert murderer."

"Hasn't murdered me yet. Fitz, he says he's a prime operator—does that mean anything to you?"

Fitz-Jones's eyebrows went up a fraction and he looked at Crowell. "That can't possibly be true. This planet's too small to rate a prime operator."

"We always send a prime when an agent gets killed," Crowell said. "No matter how unimportant the case is otherwise."

"Possibly," Fitz-Jones mused, "and if so, I am indeed honored." He gave a little mocking bow. "But the most expert bridge player would lose if he couldn't pick up his cards. That's the position you're in, sir."

"Do you know what will happen if you murder me, ambassador?"

"No 'if.' *After* we murder you . . . what, they'll send another prime operator? They'll soon run out."

"They'll quarantine this whole planet and ferret you out. You haven't got a chance."

"On the contrary, we have a very good chance—the

chance that you're lying. Which is rather large, considering your circumstances. I don't think ill of you for it, Mr. McGavin. I would do the same in your position."

"Why don't you stop gloating at him and get some rope. My arm's getting tired."

"Excellent idea." Fitz-Jones went outside and returned with a long coil.

"Finish your wine, Isaac. Come over here beside him, Kindle. If he tries anything, I don't want you to roast me along with him."

Otto expanded his chest and his biceps as Fitz-Jones wound the rope around him. An old trick and not very subtle, but Fitz-Jones didn't notice. The way he tied him up, just winding the rope around and around his body, reminded Otto that he was dealing with inexperienced amateurs, and he chastised himself again for being so careless. Why, they hadn't even searched him, though he had to admit that he had nothing more lethal than a penknife stashed away. Still, he had his hands and feet.

"We have several hours' wait, Mr. McGavin. I suggest you try to sleep." Fitz-Jones went into the kitchen and came out with Otto's laser and a soda bottle. He walked over to Otto and chopped down with the plastic bottle. Otto tried to dodge but it hit the side of his head and the room went all blue sparks and gelatin and faded away.

He had been awake, listening, for at least an hour when Fitz-Jones came over with a glass of water and poured it on his head.

"Wake up, Mr. McGavin. It's midnight, the lights are out, and we're going for a little stroll." Otto staggered to his feet, careful to puff out his chest and flex his muscles so the bonds appeared taut.

"I just thought of something, Fitz. Do you have an extra pair of nightglasses?"

"What? You didn't bring yours?"

"I'm not in the habit of carrying them around in broad daylight."

"Well, then, I'll just take care of him alone. We aren't going to take a light."

"Oh, no, you don't. After what he did to me *I* want the pleasure of roasting him—slowly."

"Sure, and stumble into a dustpit along the way. I'm *not* letting you use the glasses and go out with him alone. You couldn't hit the ground with a rock, not even right-handed."

"Fitz, he's unarmed and tied up. And he can't see in the dark."

"Unarmed and tied up and blind, he's more dangerous than you would be in command of a battle cruiser. That's the end of the discussion."

"All right, all right. Just let me come along to finish him off. I can hang onto your belt."

Fitz-Jones glanced at McGavin, who was smiling in spite of his predicament. "The arrangement has a certain lack of dignity. I can see it amuses our friend. But all right. You can walk along behind me, but if he tries anything, let me handle it."

"Sure, Fitz." He ostentatiously switched the laser to safety. "Even if he starts throwing fission bombs, I won't fire until we get there. Then let me get in front of you and find him by laser-light."

"Let's be on with it, then. Mr. McGavin, it will be your honor to lead us. I'll direct you." They went out the kitchen door into the absolute blackness of the desert.

Otto knew he had half a kilometer in which to make his move. He figured that they would be least alert about halfway there. He counted carefully measured steps, twelve hundred to a kilometer.

The men were silent except for occasional terse directions from Fitz-Jones. Otto counted three hundred steps, then moved slightly to his left. Under the rope, he raised his left hand to his right shoulder and his left arm popped out of the coil. His body shielded the action from Fitz-Jones. He had a firm mental picture of the man behind him, and could strike at any vital spot once he knew where any part of his body was.

He stopped and Fitz-Jones prodded him with the laser, giving him a reference point. He brought his left hand around in a shallow chop that sent the laser spinning, and before it hit the ground he delivered a savage, killing kick to the groin with enough force to knock both men down.

He heard the laser skitter away and ran after it as the two men fell. But on the third step he skidded on loose gravel, lost his balance, and, falling, went into a shoulder roll—but his shoulder never hit the ground.

He hit the dustpit with a faint pop and was floating through a nightmarish world of viscous powder. He fought to hold his breath as the dust crawled into his nostrils. Then his knees bumped against the rock floor of the pit. Fighting panic, he stood and pushed his free arm straight up. He couldn't tell whether his hand cleared the surface of the pit. Lungs burning, he tried to walk back the way he had fallen, then realized that his sense of direction had vanished. He tried to walk in a straight line, any direction was all right, the pit couldn't be more than a few meters in diameter; if it were bigger they would use *it* for their dumping place; but it was impossible to walk and he drifted to his knees and crawled slowly until his head pressed against the stony wall of the pit and he dragged himself upright and painfully started to pull the heavy Crowell-body up handhold foothold right arm free biceps bruising against plastiflesh eyes on fire itching have to sneeze cool breeze on hand find edge pull up freedom.

Otto put his chin on the edge of the pit, exhaled in a quick hiss and sucked in air, started to sneeze, and bit his tongue hard. Kindle was screaming.

"I can't *see!* You broke them, Goddamnit!" Fitz-Jones was moaning, little animal whimpering sounds.

Suddenly the red glare of a laser flooded the scene. Kindle was fanning it around, using it as a searchlight. That was stupid; if anyone was awake back at the Company, they'd see it. Not likely they would come out and investigate, though.

Fitz-Jones, who shouldn't even have been alive, was actually standing, staggering, doubled over with pain. The edge of the beam caressed him and one leg burst into flame. He whirled around twice and disappeared. Another dustpit.

The light flickered off. "McGavin? I hope you saw that! You're hiding out there somewhere, I know it! But I can wait, I can wait—when it gets light, you're a dead man!"

McGavin cautiously pulled himself out of the dustpit. He unwound the rope that was still wrapped loosely around his body. After investigating the ground around the pit by touch, he had to admit that Fitz-Jones's laser must have fallen in. He wasn't going after it.

There was a large outcropping of rock about thirty meters away; he had seen it by laser-light. Slowly, silently he crawled in that direction, groping in front of him, patting the ground with his palm. Several times his hand found the warm talcum-powder softness of a dustpit; he detoured around. Finally he got to the outcropping and sat behind a large boulder.

He took stock. One vibroknife, two hands, two feet, and lots of rocks. One coil of rope. He had the alternatives of garrotting Kindle, cutting him to pieces, or simply breaking every bone in his body. All of them very effective against an unarmed man. But suicide against a laser.

He was tired, more tired than he could remember having been in all of his strenuous life. He rattled the pillbox softly. *One Gravitol left, have to save it, take it just before dawn.*

He formulated and discarded half a dozen plans.

Might as well have just taken a deep breath in the dust-pit. So tired.

Footsteps—Kindle wouldn't be insane enough to walk up in the dark . . . no, too confident; it was a Bruuchian. He walked right up and sat down, not a meter away. Otto could hear his breathing.

McGavin whispered in the informal mode, "Do I know you/ friend who comes in the night?"

"Crowell-who-jests/ I am Pornuuran/ of the family Tuurlg./ You do not know me/ though I know you./ You are a friend of my brother/ Kindle-who-leads." The Bruuchian also whispered.

"Kindle-who-leads/is in your family?"

"Yes/ the priests gave the family Tuurlg/ the honor-tradition of adopting/ the highest humans/ Kindle-who-leads and/ before him/ Malatesta-the-highest."

"Brother-of-my-friend Pornuuran/ could you lead me/ from this place/ before the desert is light?"

The Bruuchian laughed, an almost silent belch. "Crowell-who-jests/ you are indeed the merriest human./ My brothers and I/ came to observe/ the human stillness ritual./ Of course we cannot interfere.

"The priests/ saw the red light in the desert/ and sent us here for instruction/ perhaps to help/ carry the still one."

"Where are your older brothers?"

"Crowell-who-jests/ my oldest and youngest brothers/ stand near their brother/ Kindle-who-leads./ He also asked us to/ lead him in darkness/ to lead him to you/ but we would not disobey/ the priests' order."

Thank God for that, Otto thought. He briefly considered using the native as a shield, but that would be pretty low. And ineffective; the native was too small.

With a start Otto realized that he could see a vague outline of the native silhouetted against the lighter rock. He took out the pillbox and swallowed his last Gravitol. Instantly the tiredness washed away.

He peered over the side of the boulder. He couldn't

yet see Kindle, but it would only be a matter of minutes; dawn came swiftly here. Then Kindle could walk up at his leisure.

Suddenly McGavin had a plan . . . it was outrageously simple, and rather risky. But it might work—and he had little choice.

Otto gathered an armload of rocks and set out across the plain, moving as quickly as he could with safety. By the time his hand found a dustpit, there was enough light that he could see it disappear into the powder. He felt around and determined where the edge was, then set down the rocks and his vibroknife and lowered himself into the warm pool, fighting the urge to scramble out immediately.

He arranged the rocks around the flat edge in such a way that his head would be hidden from view when he was immersed up to his chin.

The blade of the knife only slid out halfway when he touched the button on the side. He checked with his fingernail, and it wasn't vibrating. The dust must have fouled the mechanism. Well, it still had a point and an edge.

He could hear Kindle moving—about twenty meters away, he estimated. Still couldn't see the man, but he chucked a rock in his direction.

The laser glared in answer. It roasted the boulder he had been using as a shield; he could hear the rock crackle and smelled a sharp tang of ozone and nitrogen dioxide.

"Getting warm back there, McGavin? I know where you are—I heard my little friend go up there. Might as well just step out and save yourself the wait." He gave the rock another short burn.

Now he could just make out Kindle. There were three Bruuchians walking with him. He was stepping very cautiously, watching the ground. Otto immersed himself up to his nose.

"This is it, McGavin. Now you're a dead man." Otto

looked over the edge and saw Kindle's back some five meters away. If the knife were working, he could throw it for an easy kill. But two inches of plain steel required closer action.

He picked up the knife and quietly pulled himself out of the pit. He ran softly toward Kindle, who was shouting at the rock, laser at eye level. Almost too easy.

Then one of the Bruuchians jerked his head around, seeing Crowell. Kindle caught the movement and turned. Otto dove for his knees, to tackle him. The beam brushed Otto and his shoulder and half his face burst into flame, then snuffed out immediately as he piled into Kindle and both men went down heavily. Otto pinned his gun-arm to the ground and the ravening beam spent itself uselessly on the big rock while Otto plunged the knife again and again into Kindle's back, even in a white fury of pain and hate instinctively going for the vulnerable kidneys. The shock reactivated the knife; the rest of the blade hummed out and then it slipped with equal fluidity through flesh and bone and organs. Kindle arched his back and was still.

Otto got to his knees and saw that Kindle still held the laser in a spastic grip, doing a fair job of melting the rock. He couldn't pry the pistol from Kindle's fist, and he stopped trying as wave after wave of intense pain throbbed through his body and he remembered his training.

Still crouched over Kindle's body, he closed his eyes and repeated over and over the mnemonic that, from his hypnotraining, isolated the pain and squeezed it into a smaller and smaller space. When it was a tiny pin-prick as hot as the interior of a star, he pushed it just a millimeter outside of his skin and held it there. Very carefully he sat down and slowly released for use those parts of his mind that weren't occupied with keeping the pain outside.

He touched his face with the back of his hand and

when he withdrew it, long filaments of melted plastiflesh still clung to it. He noted that his other hand was still dripping with gore, with Kindle's life, and he felt absolutely nothing, triumph or remorse.

The material of his shirt vaporized, and the plastiflesh over his shoulder had melted completely away. The real flesh ran from angry pink to deep blistered red to a black charred mass the size of his hand. A trickle of blood oozed from the well-done area, and Otto dispassiontely decided it wasn't enough blood loss to justify bandaging the wound.

The two younger Bruuchians came out from behind the rock and stood over Kindle. The older one limped out and rattled off something in the informal mode, too fast for Otto to translate.

They picked up Kindle's stiff body and balanced it on their shoulders to carry it away like a log. Suddenly it dawned on Otto that Kindle wasn't really dead; the oldest and youngest had passed him into stillness while his knife was doing its work. He looked at the rictus of pain on the man's face and remembered Waldo's evidence.

The man was not dead, but he was dying. And he would die slowly for hundreds of years. Otto smiled.

Dr. Norman and two stretcher-bearers picked their way across the desert and got to Crowell just before noon. Thirty years of medical practice couldn't have prepared the doctor for the sight of a critically injured man sitting in front of a pool of dried and putrifying blood and gore, half his face a burned and running ruin, and the other half smiling beatifically.

REDUNDANCY
CHECK: AGE 39

Biographical check, please, go:
I was born Otto Jules McGavin on 24 Avril AC 198
Skip to age 18, please, go:
The only thing I went to university for was to get out
into space, I didn't have any talent for science or mathe-
matics so took courses that would qualify me for offplanet Confederación service.
Skip to age 33, please, go:
Took six months of PO to recover from the Bruuch
assignment, they segued me from Isaac Crowell persona
to Heart-is-sacred-to-Manson, minister plenipotentiary
on Earth from Charlie's World, infiltrating assassination
ring from the top
Skip to age 35, please, go:
New arm didn't take, had to go back into the hospital
for two months, have it amputated and regrown, then
pushed papers most of the year, then went to Sammler
as Eduardo Muenchen, supposedly a professional gam-
bler who actually coordinated espionage group from
Jardin (Article Seven violation, economic interference),
TBII liaison set me up for identity spill, had to shoot
my way out, O God, nine people dead, six of them
innocent
The new arm worked all right? Please, go:
Worked better than the old one, my God, the look on
the little girl's face

Skip to age 37, please, go:
They tried to use her as a shield, she kept looking at me while she died
Skip to age 37, please, go:
She never even looked at her wound, O God, guts spilling out, just kept staring at me while I tried to get the door
I said skip to age 37, please, go:
Right action is abstaining from killing, stealing, and
Cashew, battery.
right livelihood is earning a living
Rouge.
is earning a living in a way not harmful to any living thing. Right effort
Pulpy.
is to avoid evil thoughts and overcome them.
Now sleep.

EPISODE:

THE ONLY WAR WE'VE GOT

A uniformed aide opened the door of the TBII Personality Overlay section and stood aside as Otto McGavin crept out. He shuffled painfully, leaning on a weathered stick, the rustling of noisome rags an unpleasant counterpoint to his adenoidal panting. His nose looked—was—freshly broken, and his face and arms were covered with running sores. The aide managed without touching him to guide him through a door marked BRIEFING AND DEBRIEFING—J. ELLIS, PH.D.

Inside the office, the aide parked him on a straight-backed chair facing a nervous young man who sat in a government-gray chair behind a government-gray desk. The aide left quickly, once he was sure that his charge wasn't going to fall out of the chair.

"C-cashew," the young government man stuttered. "Battery. Rouge. P-pulpy."

A light glimmered behind the rheum in Otto's eyes and he levered himself out of the chair, staggered, and almost fell. "What . . ." He touched his face, winced, and stared at the sticky dampness on his fingers. He dropped back into the chair.

"Now this time, this time it's gone too far." He plucked at the rags and a fragment came away between his fingers. "Exactly who am I supposed to be this time . . . the Ancient Mariner? The Wandering Jew? Or just a garden-variety leper?"

"Now, Colonel McGavin, I assure you, uh . . ."

"Assure me and be damned! This is three times in a row—three times I've been some weak old cob. Somebody in Planning must want my ass dead!"

"No, no, not at all . . . that's not it at *all*." He shuffled some papers at his desk, not looking at Otto. "You have a good, uh, extremely good record of success . . . under severe PO handicap, especially—"

"So think of how much better I could do if you clowns would let me be a normal human being for a change!" He grasped his raggy left arm, almost able to encircle bicep and triceps with one bony hand. " 'PO handicap.' If you'd kept me under for another week, you'd have handicapped me into the grave."

"You know it's only, uh, temporary—"

"Temporary! Young man—"

"Dr. Ellis," he said mildly.

"Young *doctor;* it might only take me a couple of weeks starving in a null-gee field to lose all of this muscle, but I've got to get it back the old-fashioned way. Even with hypnosis—"

"No, Colonel, it *is* temporary . . . I mean . . ."

"What *do* you mean?"

"Well, you're expected to . . . recover while on the assignment. Your persona is that of a, well, you might say a professional athlete."

"Yeah, the hundred-meter crutch relay, I can—"

"But no . . . no, you don't see, he's been . . ." Ellis shuffled papers some more. "If we can get on with the briefing, I'll—"

"All right, all right. Nobody ever lets me bitch. What, I'm going to infiltrate a hospital? A health spa?"

"Oh no, no, neither. First a police station. The individual you're impersonating is in jail, awaiting sent—"

"For dripping on somebody."

"Uh, no, for murder. Premeditated first-degree murder. Assassination, actually."

"Hey, that's really fine. A new experience. Brain-wipe."

"Uh, well, you won't be on Earth, you see, uh—"

"I think I get the picture."

"On Selva they punish murderers either by burning at the stake or public cas—"

"I don't want to hear it. I don't want to *do* it."

"You have no choice, of course."

"Ah, but I do," Otto said, tensing. "All I have to do is kill you before you can—"

"Pulpy—rouge—battery—cashew!" he shouted. Otto slumped in the chair, face slack. Dr. Ellis sighed and blotted his forehead, got up, and rummaged in a file until he found a holstered laser. He beat the dust off it, sat down again, drew out the gun, and pointed it at the center of Otto's chest. "Cashew. Battery. Rouge. Pulpy."

Otto shook his head to clear it and looked down the barrel of the weapon. Quietly: "Put that Goddamn thing away before you electrocute yourself. The battery selector's on 'charge.'"

No ten-year-old would fall for that, but Dr. Ellis had evidently spent his youth in the pursuit of scholarship. He reversed the weapon to look at the power matrix, holding it very gingerly. Otto smacked it out of his hand and, not moving too swiftly, picked it up off the rug.

"Pulpy, uh . . ."

"No." Otto had the weapon shoulder-high, the muzzle of it wavering a meter from the man's nose. "Calm down."

He went back to his chair, keeping the doctor covered, and sat. He shook his head.

"You bureaucrats are really max. Really max. Can't take a joke." He tossed the gun to the doctor's desk, but it didn't quite make it. It clattered against the edge and went spinning to the floor.

"That's government property," Ellis said.

"So am I, Goddamnit." Otto leaned back and started

93

when a joint popped loudly. "So am I." He studied the doctor for a few silent seconds. "Go on. I'm this murderer . . ."

"Ah. Yes." Ellis relaxed, lacing his fingers together. "But let's not get ahead of ourselves. We have a problem on Selva."

"I gathered."

"Um, yes, it's a problem. On the level you're operating, it's a problem of murder. Of systematic assassination, really."

"So I'm an assassin."

"In a . . . manner of speaking. But the problem is much larger than that."

"I should hope."

"Yes, well, it's war."

"So? Nothing in the Charter—"

"Interplanetary war."

Otto leaned forward, smiling slightly. "Inter*plane*tary war? You're pulling my fern. Nobody—"

"I know." He sighed. "We're getting ahead of ourselves again."

"Begin at the beginning, then."

"I was going to say, yes. Do you know anything about Selvan politics?"

"Look, I can't keep up with every jerkwater—"

"All right, that's what I thought. Don't worry, your persona knows all it has—"

"Of course. Go on."

"Well, Selva is classified as an hereditary-representative oligarchy."

"Like you say, I'll know all of this."

"Patience, please. There are forty-two hereditary clans who send one representative apiece to an interclan ruling council, the *Senado Grande*. This representative is the eldest son of the head of the clan. He will eventually head up the clan himself, and send *his* son to the *Senado*."

"Just a puppet for the old man, I assume."

"Generally, yes. In practice, the *Senado* serves as a training ground, preparing the young men for the more difficult jobs waiting for them when their fathers die or step down.

"Selva doesn't have a strong central government; hasn't had one for centuries, and the *Senado* just formalizes into law agreements made between the various clan heads in secret meetings."

"Very advanced."

"Well, it works. They started out neo-Maoist . . . anyhow, here's the problem:

"On Selva, serious personal differences between adult males are generally settled by dueling—"

"Dueling!"

"Yes, it's a delightful planet. Usually they duel with swords, sometimes with more exotic weapons. The outcome of the duel usually is just a wounding—first blood wins the argument—but over serious matters they sometimes duel to the death."

"I haven't handled a sword since training! Almost twenty years—"

"That long? Well, don't worry, your persona is quite expert; the boy he murdered, he murdered with—"

"Boy? The boy he murdered?"

"He was sixteen, just a few days past his sixteenth birthday. That's the legal age limit for duels.

"Which is at the bottom of your assignment. Let me explain. The man behind this interplanetary war idea is a clan head named Alvarez. He wants to attack Grünwelt—"

"Oh, I've heard of—"

"Yes, Grünwelt is a comparatively prosperous world; unlike Selva, it has stayed in the mainstream of Confederación life. And they're practically next-door neighbors. They come as close as sixty million kilometers at opposition."

"What do they want to start a war for? Haven't they ever heard of—"

95

"October? Sure, they've heard of October. In their schools, they teach that it's a myth, that the Confederación is too spineless to ever—"

"Still, why an interplanetary war?"

Ellis shrugged. "This man Alvarez . . . well, for generations Selvans have been jealous of Grünwelt, and Alvarez is playing on this jealousy. Reduced to the simplest of terms, he proposes to swoop in and *loot* it."

"Is Grünwelt aware—"

"Only our representative there. They don't have any espionage system on Selva; they've never seen her as a potential threat. How could they? Selva has only two working interplanetary vessels, not even a Class II spaceport."

"Then how does Selva propose to—"

"That's the funny thing. They *could* do it. Sneak attack with ten, twelve small ships. Bomb a couple of cities, threaten to bomb more, collect the booty, and return. Leave a couple of ships in orbit as insurance against retaliation."

"Never work."

"I know it wouldn't work and you know it wouldn't work and I suspect that Alvarez knows, too. We can only guess at what he's actually up to."

"Power base, I suppose. He'll use the scheme to make himself top man on Selva—"

"—and then perhaps blackmail himself into a position of power on Grünwelt. Who knows? That's one thing you may be able to find out.

"The man you'll be impersonating is Ramos Guajana. You're one of four or five skilled duelists who have been systematically assassinating not those who oppose Alvarez, but the sons of that opposition."

"As soon as they turn sixteen."

"When practical." Ellis lit up a stick and passed the box to McGavin. "It's all very legal."

"I'm sure. Thanks. But question: how could this

96

wreck, Guajana, bump off anything bigger than a cock-roach?"

"Oh, you're normally in much better shape, of course. Guajana's been imprisoned for over two months—starvation diet, beatings almost daily. You'll be in good fighting trim soon after you escape."

"But first I have to starve down to where I can slip through the bars—"

"Oh, no. We have a foolproof plan." Ellis looked at his watch. "Well, you'll get more detailed orders on the ship. Put out your cigarette, we've got to—"

"There's not *that* big a rush," Otto said. He smoked slowly for a few minutes. Then he put out the stick and returned to his chair, and Ellis put him under with the sequence of nonsense words.

"When you awaken," Dr. Ellis said confidently, "you will be about ten per cent Otto McGavin and ninety per cent Ramos Guajana. Your response to any normal situation will be consistent with Guajana's personality and abilities: only in times of extreme emergency will you be able to call upon your skills as a prime operator.

"Pulpy. Rouge. Battery. Cashew." He pushed a call button under his desk.

Guajana/Otto shook his head twice and looked across the desk with clear eyes full of pain. His face had changed in subtle ways.

"I will remember you, doctor," he croaked with a heavy accent.

2

MISSION PROFILE

NAME: Guajana, Ramos Mario Juan Federico
AGE: 39   SEX: M   MAR STAT: Div
BIRTHPLACE: Paracho, Stvo. Or., Selva
ADDRESS: Currently detained at Cerros Verdes

Clinico Psych'o, awaiting trial for 1st-degree murder.

EDUC: Equiv 1–2 yr college

PROF: Dueling master

DIST PHYS CHAR: Body and face covered with dueling scars (see accompanying chart); presently showing effects of severe beating, lack of medical treatment.

AGENT: McGavin, Otto (S–12, prime)

PHYSICAL/CULTURAL DIVERGENCE INDEX:

	SUBJECT	AGENT	INDEX
HGT.	174 cm	175 cm	—
WGT.	62 kg	80 kg	.98
AGE	40 (T)	39 (T)	.99
STP.	J.101M.024K.039	J.090M.036K.021	.80
LNG.	Selvan (var Sp)	Eng (LI.98)	.99
PPRF.	AG.95H.46L.05–	AG.83H.79L——–	
	PT.88LA.68LY.90–	PT.72LA.78LY.68–	
	AN.32SH.11D.89	AN.41SH.75D.88	.82

OVERALL 0.86

PO SCALE: 0.99

TIME SURG: 3d, 4hr

TIME PO: 24d, 12hr

And there were over a hundred pages after that. It was the only thing to read in the crowded cabin of the tiny T–46, and in the four weeks it took to get to Selva, Otto/Guajana read it over completely sixty-three times.

Most of it detailed Otto's mission. From past experience, he knew that ninety-nine per cent of the planning would be worthless after the first day or two. And as far as the reams of data about the man he was impersonating . . . normally that would also be useless; if he ever had to consciously *act* like the man, it would mean his PO was fading and he would soon have to fight or run for his life.

But most personality overlays are done in hypnotic rapport between the agent and the person he is going to impersonate. In this case that had been impossible; Guajana couldn't be kidnapped for a month and have his copy remain of any use. So they had examined and profiled Guajana as well as possible, and Otto was a very good academic copy of the man. He lacked the important artificial memories that would have been overlaid in hypnotic rapport—but then he could make a good case for having been beaten into amnesia.

So Otto memorized all of the information about Guajana, just in case, which was not too pleasant: Guajana was about the most villainous person Otto had ever impersonated. Cold-blooded murderer of children, for hire. Well, maybe he had a good side. Kind to snakes or something.

It was a cloudy, absolutely starless night when Otto landed on Selva in a small clearing in the mountainous jungle that surrounded Cerros Verdes. His timing was very bad.

The T–46 is about as automated as a spaceship can be. It locks in on a landing signal—generated in this case by Otto's TBII liaison—and casts about for the nearest thirty-meter stretch of level ground on which to land. But the signal in this case was being generated from the top of a steep hill in the middle of a rain forest so up-and-down that it would drive a cartographer insane.

The ship glided to a stop and Otto pulled from a pocket of his rags a simple signal-detector/rangefinder that told him he was 12.8 kilometers south-southeast of where he wanted to be. A small error in a 45-light-year journey, but Otto/Ramos was understandably upset.

As noted, the T–46 is very automatic: automatic to a fault. Its function is to land an agent safely and get away

—its door opens and the agent has sixty seconds to clear out or be automatically ejected. Otto was upset because the hundred-page report had stressed that only rabid sportsmen and other madmen dared venture into Selvan jungles at night.

Otto got out and felt the ship depart silently behind his back. Laser ready, with his left hand he adjusted his nightglasses and tightened the shoulder straps of his kit. He looked around and saw nothing but then felt a crawly sensation center on his back and whirled.

At neck level and ten meters away a batlike creature with a three-meter wingspan and an excessive number of claws and teeth was sliding rapidly through the air with a bloodthirsty grin on what served it for a face. It seemed to weigh about as much as a human child, and it screamed like a child when the laser opened it up in mid-flight. It tumbled suddenly graceless over Otto's head to crash in the tall grass behind him, where it thrashed twice. There was a second's stillness and then a slithering sound and then the crunch of strong jaws crushing bone.

In the flare of the laser, Otto had seen a hundred pairs of hungry eyes. There was no way to whistle the ship back.

It may be better in some absolute sense to accept a known danger, however great, than to forge off into the unknown. Otto knew that the woods probably held a more interesting variety of fauna than this small veldt— but he'd feel safer with a thick tree at his back. He checked his direction bump against the small rangefinder and set off north by northwest.

Twice in ten steps Otto fired at nothing. He cursed himself for nervousness, for wasting power, and then on the twelfth step a red snake with a head the size of a man's and eyes that actually did glow lunged for Otto's belt buckle. After the laser severed its head, the body coiled and writhed through eight long meters of grass.

For all the years of training and conditioning and experience, Otto suddenly had no control over the toroidal muscle that makes elimination a polite and private function. His anal sphincter bucked and spasmed in that final reflex that tries to make a trapped creature an unpleasant meal. There was no room in his mind for thankfulness that he had taken the elementary precaution that kept him from fouling himself—there was nothing in his head but primitive panic from ear to ear and he screamed and ran blindly for two seconds, hit dirt in a flat dive, rolled, and came up firing. The laser's beam made a brilliant arc swinging back and forth in front of him, then behind, saving his life as it killed the bat-creature's mate. When he took his finger off the trigger the glade was in crackling flames that dimmed and smoldered out in the dampness. At the edge of the woods something gave a bad imitation of a human laugh and Otto's self-preserving panic reached so high a level that it flipped the final mental switch the conditioners had put into his brain and he was suddenly ice:

McGavin, you are going to die.

I know that, McGavin.

What do you do before you die?

Kill as many as I can.

There is a theory, not provable, that no creature in the Galaxy is more dangerous than man. At any rate, few men could be as dangerous as one who has given up all hope for his own survival—add to that half a lifetime of experience in bloody murder and you may have the only kind of man who could survive three hours alone at night in a Selvan jungle.

The fact that nighttime is so hostile on Selva was the single most important influence on the strange evolution of Selvan politics. The planet was originally colonized by five hundred idealistic volunteers from the Terran country of Uruguay, members of the Programa Político de Mao, who had bought the planet cheaply from a mining corporation that couldn't find anybody willing to run their machines.

El Programa arrived with a nice efficient setup, a division of duties and rewards that might have worked very well in a more hospitable environment.

The mining company had not totally misled them about the danger of Selva—they came with guns and electric fences and grim determination and absolutely no desire to go near the jungle at night. But to the planet they were just so many relatively accessible pieces of protein dropped in the middle of about the most competitive land ecology ever discovered—twenty-five thousand kilograms of monster meat.

They lost nearly a hundred members the first day and the same number in the week that followed. The next week forty vanished, then seventeen, and then eight.

It might be naïve to infer that a primitive kind of natural selection was going on, that only the toughest survived. There may have been some element of that, but far more important was the factor of simple luck and practice. They had all been farmers by profession— and temperament—and no farmer, however tough, could know enough about knee-jerk killing to stay alive long on Selva—except by luck. If he lived and learned he eventually needed less luck—although he became a less pleasant neighbor.

Inexorably, in less than one generation, what had been intended as a gentle experiment in communal living degenerated into a bizarre association of mutually suspicious clans, a system more appropriate to the fourteenth century than the twenty-third.

It started with the status of women. In El Programa, women were supposed to have been absolutely equal to men, except for performing the special function of childbirth. To keep the colony from becoming inbred, the planters had included ten thousand sets of sperm and egg, ready for quickening; all of the expedition's men had allowed themselves to be sterilized. With what were then considered modern medical techniques, a woman could give birth in four to five months after implantation.

By the time the population had stabilized at around two hundred, it was obvious that every female would have to be kept pregnant every day for the rest of her life, until her womb cried uncle, or the race would wither on the vine. And she had to be protected from Selva, which was virtually a sentence of life imprisonment with time off for old age.

At first the women were kept in the five colonizing vessels, now useless as transportation but proof against teeth and claws. The men stayed with them at night and ventured out during the day to hunt, which was easy, and to try to farm, which was rather difficult with one eye and one hand otherwise occupied.

After some ten years they did manage to build high fortifications around each ship. The electric fences, which had proved useless before because dead creatures would just pile up and eventually make a bridge, were unraveled and restrung as barriers against the gliding monsters.

Population pressure shoved the walls outward as the years went by. The people lived first in capsules, then stockades, then forts, and finally in walled towns. Eventually five towns grew together to form the sprawling city of Castile Cervantes.

There were schools, but they taught a minimum of academic subjects and a maximum of how to stay alive.

Most of the first generation still considered themselves communists. The second generation thought communism was ridiculous. The third generation was sentimental about it, and by the tenth generation very few people knew what it was.

With the women locked away like precious jewelry and the men spending half their waking hours in the expectation or dispensation of bloody murder, it was not surprising that an ugly form of social organization should develop. Since strength and ruthlessness were the only survival traits, the strongest and most ruthless went to the top and made their own rules.

They conquered their own planet in three hundred years. When they started looking for other worlds to conquer, they broke one of the very few interplanetary laws—and the Confederación, through its clandestine TBII arm, sent one man to check out the situation.

Otto McGavin was still alive when dawn broke and the miscellaneous uglies tromped or slithered or flopped or flapped back to their holes and caves.

He sat exhausted in the middle of a wide circle of burned, bizarre-looking meat. That was what had saved him. He hadn't had to fire a single shot in the past hour —Selva's night foragers naturally preferred a freshly dead meal to going to the trouble of killing the new one that spat fire.

When the sun cleared the top of the jungle canopy Otto saw no sign of life in either the jungle or the clearing. Finally feeling safe, he automatically slipped back into the Ramos Guajana personality. He shook a fist at the dead creatures and shouted a joyful curse. Then he removed the sheath knife from the side of his kit, sliced a chunk of thigh from one of a creature's six, and cheerfully munched on it as he plunged into the jungle.

At Ramos's normal walking speed, he could cover 12.8 kilometers in a comfortable hour and a half. But jungle trails are slow going and it was nearing dusk— Ramos was starting to get worried—when he broke into a clearing at the base of a steep hill. A handsome brick-and-stone building, evidently a lodge of some sort, sat on the top of the hill. Halfway up the hill a moat protected a substantial wall topped with electric webbing. He followed the path up the hill to the moat. A steelite drawbridge lowered and Ramos, wake-up jungle noises at his back, hurried across it. Another steelite door inside and the drawbridge rose behind him, trapping him in a small area.

"I am not programmed to admit you," a metallic voice said, "and the proprietress is not at home to identify you." A light came on in a little alcove to his left. "You are protected from the night, however, and there are sanitary facilities and food machines to your left." There sure were—all coin-operated. All he had was in large bills—and counterfeit at that.

"Can you change a fifty?" he asked the machine.

"Repeat, please."

"Can you change a fifty?"

"I am not programmed to admit you—"

"Oh, shut up!" That was evidently in its programming—it shut up.

When he picked the lock on the toilet the light went out.

He napped for an hour or so on a bench behind the useless sandwich machine. A small noise—the door being unlocked—woke him up; he took cover behind the machine and centered his laser on where he thought the door was. The nightglasses were packed away in his kit.

"Guajana," a female voice said, "Ramos Guajana?"

"Sí. *Aqui*." His contact, R. Eshkol, was a woman? On this planet?

"Oh, there you are." She walked toward him. "Put away that gun and take my hand. I'll guide you up to the place."

They walked up a steep path. "I've been out in a flyer, looking for you," she said. "I discovered where you spent the night. Very impressive, especially without nightglasses."

He didn't say anything.

How many months since he had been this close to a woman? His hand sweated, clammy in her warm soft one; he felt wave after wave of sexual tension, so acute it affected stomach more than loins, every time he stumbled into a rounded hip or backside.

"Hey, cob. Keep your hands to yourself."

"Mierde, no veo," he growled. With effort: "Sorry. I can't see."

"Uh-huh. Well, we're almost there." As they neared the top, Ramos could barely make out a gray bulk looming.

"Here we are." She stopped and worked a heavy-sounding iron lock. "Teh Vista Hermosa Hotel. 'Hotel of the beautiful view,' " she translated needlessly. "Went out of business twenty years ago—watch your step—and the Confederación bought it through proxies." They were inside, walking over a musty-smelling carpet.

"For such an emergency as this?"

"No, it's . . . pretty simple; they thought for a while that the *Senado* was moving to Paracho, wanted a cheap place for a consulate. Got stuck with it. Stairs." Ramos hit the first tread as she said that; stumbled and, groping, found her calf.

He touched her again standing up, and she showed her affection with a stinging slap.

Coolly, Ramos grabbed her wrist and twisted her off balance. He fell on top of her, pinning her under his knees, and pressed the muzzle of the pistol to her throat, swearing gutturally. He snapped the safety off and then slowly clicked it back on. He stood up.

"Sorry. Please remember. I *am* Ramos Guajana."

She regained her feet with a rustling of full skirts. Her voice quavered. "I know. But I am what *I* am, too. On Shalom we . . . don't *touch* people that way!"

Nothing to say, Ramos shifted the pack on his back noisily.

She sighed. "Give me your hand. It's not much farther."

They went to the top of the stairs and down a corridor to the left. The door to Otto's quarters opened noiselessly and closed with a solid snap.

"Thumbprint lock. We'll reset it." The lights came on, dazzling.

The windowless room had three pieces of cheap furniture: an airbed in one corner and a wooden desk and chair in another. A small holo cube on the desk showed the inside of a cell where a man was sleeping. By the desk was a rack holding seven swords. Ramos crossed to it and ran his fingers lightly along the blades. "Adequate," he said. He pulled one out of the rack and made a few passes at an imaginary foe. Then he looked closely at the sword.

"I'll need a whetstone and a leather strop. And a roll of tape for these handles. Black tape, the kind electricians use." For the first time, he looked up and saw the girl.

"Uh . . ." By the standards of Shalom, she was a plain-looking woman. Which meant she was perhaps less perfect of figure and feature than Helen of Troy. She was dressed the way young women all dressed in this part of Selva; a clinging velvety bodice revealing only the tops of her breasts, clasping her body down to just pass the hipbones, swelling out into a full ruffled skirt, long by Earth standards.

Considering that nine-tenths of him had been three times jailed for rape, and ten-tenths had been locked up in a tiny T-46 for weeks, Ramos reacted in a fairly gentlemanly way: he dropped the sword, snarled, and took three steps toward her, clutching—

And from an intimate place she produced a small black pistol. "Now you stay right where you are!" she said, more hysteria than menace in her voice. But it was quite obvious that she was going to burn him down in another second, and the sense of immediate danger put Otto in full control of the body.

His own pistol was lying on top of his kit, which he had dropped from his back in the center of the room. If she was any kind of a marksman, she could hit him

107

five or six times before he'd be able to reach it. He put his hands on top of his head.

"Now, now," he said. "Don't get excited, it's just—heh, well—you know . . ."

"It's like they say," she said, a little more calmly, curiously. "You're actually two people."

"That's correct." He bowed slightly at the waist, hands still on top of his head. "Otto McGavin, at your service."

"Well, you better stay 'Otto McGavin' for a while." She lowered the pistol. "What a strange name you've—"

Ramos dropped his hands to his side, in claws, and was inching forward. She brought up the pistol again and he raised his hands, more slowly this time.

"Can't you control yourself for just one second?"

"Calm, please, calm down now . . . uh . . . no, actually, really, I can't, well, exactly *control* it. When I'm not in immediate danger I have to automatically act like Guajana. Otherwise I might accidentally, you know, act out of character."

She was backing toward the door. "Well, don't think for a second you're going to act *in* character with *me*." Hand on the knob. "I don't think we'll reset the lock after all. Not until I figure out what to do with you." She snapped off the lights, jumped through the door, and slammed it behind her.

A fraction of a second later, Ramos crashed into the locked door. *"Cago en la leche de la madre de su madre!"* he raged. He pounded on the door with his fists, cursing more loudly and ever more imaginatively for a few minutes. Then he walked heavily across the dark room and felt his way to the bed.

3

"Wake up, McGavin, Guajana; whatever your name is." Ramos snapped awake and looked around but there was no one in the room. Then he saw her small image in the holo cube.

"Goat bitch," he said illogically, sneering, "I no longer desire you. Set me free that I might go find a female of my own species."

She sniffed contemptuously. "Sooner or later, you'll be free enough. Right now, there's work to be done." She faded away and was replaced by the image of the real Ramos Guajana, sitting in his cell. The resemblance to Otto/Ramos was fairly exact.

Her voice over Ramos's image: "Notice that he has a new lump on his head and a healing cut on his lip. He got these fighting with a guard day before yesterday.

"We have orders saying you must watch him as near perfectly as possible before you can begin your mission. It would be dangerous to risk cosmetics, of course, so we are going to have to inflict similar injuries on—"

"Please come and try."

"That won't be necessary. Not me personally, anyhow."

The door to his quarters swung open, and a big ugly specimen stood there with a gun in one hand and a padded club in the other.

"Sorry, Colonel McGavin," he said, raising the gun. "Anesthetic." He fired as Otto tensed to leap.

Ramos woke up with a pulsating ache in his head and a swollen, stinging lip. He counted teeth with his tongue; they were all there, but a couple were loose.

"There's some analgesic in the desk drawer, Colonel." The man who had put him to sleep and, presumably, knocked him around while he was unconscious was still in the room. Or again in the room; he'd gotten rid of the gun and the club. He was sitting against the far wall with two swords and two clear plastic helmets.

"Call me Ramos," he said, going to the desk. Standing up and walking produced a sensation not unlike that of having someone probe his temple with an ice pick.

109

Ramos touched the side of his head and closed his eyes for a second, tried to ignore the pain, and failed.

He took the pill and touched his lip gingerly. "I suppose I should thank you. Do you render this service often?"

"Not for cosmetic purposes." He stood up. "Thought you might like to go a couple of rounds. These are practice swords, épées." He tossed one to Ramos, who caught it by the handle without effort.

"You feel up to it?"

"I suppose." Actually, Ramos/Otto felt a thousand per cent better, even with the new lumps, than he had in Dr. Ellis's office on Earth. The personality overlay people had had to overdo the damage to his body to allow for healing during the four weeks' transit. He wasn't up to normal pitch for either Guajana or McGavin, but he had some measure of strength and swiftness back.

"Frankly," the big man said while Ramos tested the balance and temper of the weapon, "I'm skeptical. I don't see how they can teach you in a few weeks what it took Guajana most of his life to master."

Ramos shrugged. "It's only temporary." He sized up the other man. He moved with a grace that seemed almost effeminate for a man of his size. He had all of the physiological advantages for fencing: taller than Ramos by a head and a half, long arms and legs. But Ramos knew that people with a long reach and a long lunge tended to get overconfident with a small opponent. It would be fun, setting him up for the kill.

Ramos adjusted the helmet, a good porous plastic shield that protected his face and ears and throat.

"I'll take it easy at first," the other man said.

"No need." They took up *garde* positions in the center of the room. Ramos noted that his opponent's blade was canted out of line to the right by more than two centimeters, exposing a little too much shoulder and forearm. His opponent either had bad form or had set up a trap, not a terribly subtle one. Without thinking about it, Ramos executed an attack that would take care of either alternative—in one motion feinting to the exposed forearm, slipping under the expected parry, then double-disengage (bell guard high for this line against the possibility of stop thrust or out-of-time remise), *lunge,* and the blunted point thumped to rest precisely between the third and fourth ribs.

"*Tocar,*" the big man acknowledged, fingering thoughtfully the spot where he had been touched. "I'll have to be more careful."

He *was* more careful, and very good by anybody's standards, but in five engagements Ramos scored five touches. None of the clashes lasted more than a few seconds; the longest was attack-parry-riposte-parry-remise-parry-reremise-touch.

"Very strange." The man took off his mask. "Colonel, uh, Ramos, I mean . . . you say they taught you how to fence like Guajana?"

"That's right."

"But I've fenced with Guajana—hundreds of times! —and . . ."

"And you're still alive?"

"No, no, not dueling. He was my coach five, six years ago. That's why—anyhow, you don't really fence much like him . . . a casual opponent wouldn't see it, but I know where his weaknesses are; I've even beaten him a few times. You don't have those weaknesses, not those particular ones."

"Ah." Ramos's brow furrowed, searching his memory of the mission profile. "Well, it's understandable. I had to get it secondhand, since the real Guajana was stuck here. They got the best fencing masters they could find —Italy, Hungary, France—"

"All the way from France!"

"No, not the planet; those are countries on Earth. They got these masters and had them study tapes of Guajana at work. Then the masters taught me in tan-

111

dem, simultaneously, all of us under hypnosis. So I got imprinted with a kind of average impression of Guajana's style.

"Complicated," the man said. "But easy, compared to learning the real way. I'm glad it doesn't last."

"I wish it could last a little longer. I've got to wrap up this project before the imprinting starts to fade. Two months at the very most."

"Anything I can do to help, of course—"

"No. Don't even say it. You don't want to help; you don't even want to *know* anything more about this than you do now. Same goes for that bitch—"

"Rachel?" He looked hurt. "But . . . she's the TBII liaison."

"Something this backwoods planet shouldn't even *have!* I never feel safe on an assignment where somebody else knows my true identity. People have a nasty way of being compelled to talk. So far, two of you know who I am. How many others—the whole embassy staff?"

"No, we're the only two."

"Then the best thing you could do for me, both of you, would be to get offplanet. Right now."

"Mr. Guajana," came a thin voice, Rachel's from the cube, "try to remember that we are the officially appointed representatives of the Confederación on this planet. You are only a tool, a specialist sent to aid *us* in the resolution of this problem. It's still our respons—"

"You know, I don't give a flying—" Ramos stopped, continued in a lower voice: "Deep down inside, I don't really *care* whether Selva builds a thousand warships and blasts Grünwelt back to the Stone Age. I would never even have *heard* of Selva if your Alvarez hadn't come down with an Attila complex." Normally, Guajana remembered vaguely, he was very polite and suave with ladies.

"Then I wouldn't say that you were ideally motivated for your job," she said scornfully. "Don't you have even a little sympathy for—"

"Sympathy, motivation, *mierde*." He took a deep breath and tried to calm down. "Sympathies can change and motivation is a simple word for something nobody understands. I do a good job, the best job I can, because I've been conditioned down to the last brain cell and stringy nerve to complete my mission. I am totally reliable because nobody but the TBII has the knowledge and equipment to break my conditioning."

"You are a thoroughly despicable person."

"Because I pinched your butt, big deal. Big f—"

"Please!" The big man was patting the air with both hands, conciliatory. "Rachel, nobody questions your motivation and Colonel, nobody questions your conditioning. Why don't we just *drop* all this and get down to the problem at hand?"

"One little matter first," Ramos said, still fuming. "I know who Rachel Eshkol is; she was identified in my orders—but who the hell are you?"

"Octavio de Sanchez. I work for the embassy."

"Well, I'm glad she didn't just pick you off the street. What do you do at the embassy when you're not dabbling in espionage?"

"Well, ah, I'm a data analyst for the Vital Statistics section."

"And how does this qualify you to be in on our little secret?"

"I needed somebody," Rachel began.

"You didn't even need your*self!*"

"I needed somebody of unimpeachable loyalty who knew Guajana well. To check your disguise, your acting."

"*Who's acting?* What disguise? I . . . am . . . Ramos . . . Guajana."

"He talks just like him," Octavio said.

"See?" Ramos threw up his hands. "For this you doubled my risk of exposure."

113

"Señor de Sanchez is absolutely trustworthy." Her image in the cube was leaning forward, flushed with anger.

"Oh, you want to get into *that* orbit . . . Octavio, old sport, if I offered you a million P's to go over to Alvarez's side—"

"No. He is too unutterably—"

"Two million? Five? Ten? Your life? To keep your children from being tortured to death? Your mother?"

"Yes, I see. Of course. If the price was dear enough, any man would—"

"Any man or woman on this planet—except me."

Silence for a few seconds. "Then why don't you just get rid of us . . . mere mortals," Rachel said.

"I considered it," Ramos snapped. "And I *didn't* reject it just because I thought you might be of some use to me later on. You won't be."

"Then why not just kill us?"

"Or try," Octavio added, flexing the practice sword.

"For one thing, it would draw unnecessary attention to the operation. For another, even Ramos, the real Ramos, isn't totally amoral. Certainly not impractical— he doesn't go around killing people for sport, or just because their existence inconveniences him."

"He's killed sixteen people," Octavio said grimly.

"Seventeen. But always for what he would consider good reason, or at least sufficient profit." *I've killed more than that,* Otto thought, *just to keep the Confederación running smoothly.* "Granted, he might require less reason than you would."

Octavio nodded. "Look, we're still getting nowhere. Hadn't we best go over the plan, coordinate our—"

"The plan is unworkable and is rejected as of *now*. Kidnapping Ramos and sneaking me into his cell, then having me escape . . . that's the kind of Goddamn comic opera thing Planning always dreams up."

"But we have orders—" Rachel said firmly.

"Look at the rank of the man who signed those orders

114

and then consider my rank. The TBII may not be terribly efficient, but in some ways they aren't stupid . . . the only reason I have any military rank at all is to keep people like you from hamstringing me."

"What's *your* plan, then?" she said. "How is it any better?"

"The less you know, the better for both of us. You may do two things for me and then, Octavio, you can go back to your statistics and Señorita Eshkol can go back to . . . whatever she does for fun."

"That suits me fine," she said with heat. "The sooner you get out of my life, the happier I'll be."

"What would you like us to do, Colonel?"

Ramos smiled at the cube for a second and turned back to Octavio. "First, get me reliable, inconspicuous transportation to Clan Alvarez. I suppose that would be a horse." *They make noises about interplanetary war and still use draft animals to get around on.* "Then, when I'm ready to leave, get rid of the real Ramos."

"Kill him?"

"That would be safest. Use your own judgment."

"You are forgetting that Señor Sanchez and I are not casual murderers. We'll kidnap him as planned before and lock him up in the room you're in now."

"All right. I advise you to take out the swords first."

When Octavio left, Ramos flopped down on the bed with a sigh of relief. It was hard work, trying to think like Otto and be Ramos at the same time.

Starting tomorrow, he would have to move fast. A pity: he would've liked to supervise the abduction. Perhaps the prisoner would be killed, trying to escape.

Thinking more like Ramos now, that's good.

4

To get to Clan Alvarez, Ramos had to go over two hundred kilometers, through Clans Tueme and Amarillo.

It took him two full days, riding the spavined nag Octavio had supplied him with. The second time he stopped for rest (and recreation), at an inn just across the Amarillo–Alvarez border, the prostitute he hired turned out to have known Ramos for years. She remarked about how gentle he'd suddenly become, but seemed relieved rather than suspicious.

What other important aspects of Guajana's life did the PO section know absolutely nothing about? Ramos hoped his amnesia story would cover him.

He had called the Vista Hermosa before crossing the Tueme border, and Octavio had told him that the abduction had gone smoothly, according to plan. No violence; just a certain amount of money passed around, some personnel suddenly transferred. Guajana was safely locked away in the hotel. There was a reward out for his recapture, but the physical description on the notice was inaccurate. The ruse would work for two days (until a new poster, with picture, could be issued), which gave him plenty of time to get safely into Clan Alvarez.

It was a tiring way to travel. Except in some of the larger towns, which had stone or macadam streets, most of the roads were crushed gravel. Every time a non-equine transport passed, it would pepper Ramos with a shower of pebbles and raise a cloud of stringent dust that would take several minutes to settle in the hot still air. The big ground-effect trucks, which passed about every half hour, were especially diverting, giving Ramos a nice familiarity with the jungle. He learned from one painful experience that horse and rider had to get behind a couple of meters of bush when one of the huge vehicles lumbered by; that or die a slow death by flaying in one day's journey.

By the time he reached Castile Alvarez, Ramos was covered with a half centimeter of crusted dust, aching with scratches from thorns and flung pebbles, and nearly paralyzed with saddle sores. He left his horse at a public stable, soaked for an hour in a hot tub, had his larger wounds treated, bought a rough massage and a new suit of clothes, and walked slightly bowlegged to the castle.

The castle was an airy fantasy of glass and polished steelite—obviously rather new, although more than a century out of date by the architectural standards of more civilized planets. Guarding the front gate were two pairs of men with crossed pikes, trying not to look uncomfortable in their foppish, archaic uniforms. Their armament was more ornamental than functional, but it was backed up by two megawatt-class lasers in shiny steelite bunkers flanking the road. A sign directed visitors to a small dome beside one of the bunkers. The laser's large green eye tracked Otto as he passed in front of it.

Inside, the dome had brick-red walls with black tile underfoot and what looked like a tiny woman seated at a miniature desk across from the entrance. In the subdued light it was hard to see the faint cube lines, but it was obviously a holographic projection.

The woman was plain and efficient-looking. "Please give me your name and the name of the department or person with whom you have business."

"My name is Ramos Mario Guajana. I believe I am to see el Alvarez."

"Oh . . . no, sir, that's quite impossible." She looked at him expectantly. Ramos just looked back.

"Just a moment, please." She tapped out something on the keyboard in front of her. "That's Guajana with an 'a'?"

"Yes." She tapped some more and watched a screen to her right.

"Oh—Major Guajana, you are supposed to report directly to Commandante Rubirez . . . does he have a regular office?"

"Uh . . . I don't know." 'Major' Guajana? Another

117

little detail that Planning had missed; he was a field-grade officer.

"Let me see whether I can trace him." She played with the keyboard some more and talked quietly into a microphone.

"Commandante Rubirez is in the Library, in the Rare Books Room," she said with a tone of dismissal.

"Where's that?"

"Pardon me?" Furrowed brow, cocked head.

"Look, I'm a field operative; I don't know my way around this town. Where is the library?" With exaggerated simplicity, she told him: south half of the sixth floor of the castle.

Ramos tried, with his newly discovered majorhood, to pull rank on the palace guards when they asked for his sword. The captain of the guard coldly informed him that the palace guard was outside the military's chain of command and he could surrender his sword or be burned on the spot. He handed it over. A metal detector bleated as he walked through the gate; they got his pistol, too.

Tangy cold inside the palace. Ramos realized it was the first air-conditioned air he had breathed since getting out of the little T–46. The first floor was all expensive woods and plush carpeting; mediocre paintings alternated with floor-to-ceiling mirrors. Too much empty space—it was an arrangement that owed less to esthetic than to easy defense. Any or each of those mirrors could conceal a squad of armed men. Alone on the acre-sized rug, Ramos felt a hundred eyes on him.

The elevator "boy" wore the palace guard uniform and was armed with short sword and laser pistol. He didn't say a word to Ramos, and already knew where he was going.

There was only one other person in the main room of the library, a clerk filing tapes behind a desk. He was also armed. Ramos was getting the feeling that everybody in the castle was armed except TBII agents.

"Which way to the Rare Books Room, *amigo?*"

The clerk took off old-fashioned spectacles and blinked at Ramos. "You can't go in there. Occupied."

"I know." Ramos drummed his fingers on the desk top. "I have an appointment with the Commandante."

"Ah. This way." The clerk led Ramos through a labyrinth of tape files, periodical racks, bookcases. They came to a door marked with a single 'B,' "Just a moment." He rapped on the door and opened it slightly.

"I told you I was not to be disturbed," came a frosty voice from inside.

"A gentleman says he has an appointment with you, Commandante."

"I don't have any appointments with anybody." The clerk was a surprisingly fast draw; he had the pistol steady on Ramos's breastbone before the Commandante said "any."

"I'll get rid of him, sir."

"Wait," Ramos said, almost shouting. "I'm Ramos Guajana."

"Ramos?" A book snapped shut; sound of papers rustling and heavy footsteps muffled by carpet. A bear-like head thrust itself from behind the door at a surprising height.

"Ramos," he growled with what might pass for affection. "Put that gun away, fool; Alvarez should have two such good men." Two long strides and he enveloped Ramos in a crushing embrace. Then he held him by the shoulders and studied him, head wagging back and forth, looking more ursine all the time.

"They have used you poorly, old friend."

"Not as poorly as they might have, Commandante. I was to be hanged." He shuddered, sincerely. "Or worse."

"Commandante?" He took Ramos by the arm; steered him into the Rare Books Room. "When was I other than Julio to you?"

"Sir . . . Julio . . . that's another thing. They beat me regularly, severely—"

"That's evident."

"—and I seem to have lost my memory. All memories of the past ten years or so." He lowered himself into an easy chair. "This seemed to be the logical place to go after I escaped, from the nature of their questioning." He took a chance. "I do vaguely remember . . . you."

A shadow, perhaps doubt, passed over the Commandante's bearded face, then was gone. "And well you should." He chuckled, turned around abruptly, and scanned the leather-bound volumes lining the wall. He selected a thick book titled *Philosophical Discourses,* held it to his ear, and shook it. It gurgled pleasantly. "Philosophy is the highest music," he quoted in Spanish; then he removed a bottle and two glasses from the hollow book and decanted a healthy portion of brandy into each glass. He handed one to Ramos.

"Grünweltische Branntwein. This is—" he checked the label—"Eisenmacher '36. It might be well to start developing a taste for it."

Ramos held up his glass. "We will fill swimming pools with it." They laughed and drank.

"Then you remember something of the Plan?"

Ramos shrugged. "No more than is common knowledge. My captors—is that the right word?—in Tueme implied that my killing that boy had something to do with it. I also got the impression that they were not too much in favor of the Plan."

"Not yet," he said. "But we can bring them around. Or do without them. We've gotten the support of Diaz now, much more important. Heavy industry." He stood up abruptly.

"But we can talk about this later. You must be tired." *More curious than tired,* Ramos thought, but best not to press too much.

120

He nodded. "It was an arduous journey."

"See Teniente Salazar down at the officers' billets. I'll call and make sure you get a good place."

"I'd be grateful."

"And . . . ah! Would you crave . . . feminine companionship?"

"In a relaxed sort of way, yes. My most urgent desires I satisfied at various inns between Tueme and here."

Julio clapped Ramos on the back—gently—and laughed. "Some things they could not change."

5

Ramos found that his rank—which was new, Teniente Salazar told him—entitled him to his choice of private quarters. There were only two billets available, though. Ramos took the second, even though it seemed more subtly bugged, because it was cleaner and he was expecting company. A girl named Ami Rivera; Julio had said they'd been close, before. He would warn her about his indisposition.

A clerk brought over a duffle bag of personal effects belonging to the real Guajana. Ramos found out disappointingly little about himself from the items in the bag. There were swords: blunted épée, saber, and foil for practice; functional saber and épée. Three sets of clothes, civilian. No uniforms. An opened package of pistol targets. Three books from the castle library; one of short stories and two on fencing theory (these were bound technical journals; Ramos looked for his own name but didn't find it). The only thing that didn't have some practical use was a beat-up harmonica with no upper octave. There was also a little bag of things evidently dumped from a desk drawer—anonymous stationery, pencil stub, eraser, two dried-out pens, postage stamps stuck together, a half-smoked box of dope-sticks but no matches.

Maybe the TBII's Sherlock section could comb through this collection and tell you everything from Guajana's ring size to his preference in women. To Ramos, to Otto McGavin, after an hour of close inspection, it was still just five swords, three sets of clothes, and a bunch of kipple. Anything he could infer from that he already knew.

Ami came by about sundown and fixed Ramos *timorlinos secos,* a regional seafood specialty. She was a laughing, worldly, handsome woman about Ramos's age. He enjoyed talking with her and making love with her, and never could decide whether she'd been sent to spy on him.

The next night was a slim young thing named Cecelia who had rather more exotic tastes than Ami but didn't talk much. The third night it was one Private Martinez, rather dumpy and male besides, who had been sent to bring Ramos to the Commandante's billet.

Ramos had anticipated just a larger version of his own austere quarters, but Julio's "billet" was a rambling stucco mansion in the shape of a squared U, built around a carefully tended garden.

Julio was in the garden, sitting under a large tree at a table covered with papers. A bright lantern hanging from a branch above him hissed softly and threw a circle of soft yellow light around him; the smell of its burning mixed pleasantly with the perfumes of the garden. Julio was scribbling rapidly and didn't hear Ramos and the private approach. The private cleared his throat, signalling.

"Ah! Major Guajana. Sit, sit." He waved at a chair across the table from him and went back to his writing. "I'll only be a moment. Private, find the cook and bring us some wine and cheese."

After a minute he laid the pen down with a slap and

gathered the papers together. "Ramos," he said, stacking the pages, "if they ever offer you a colonelcy, turn it down. It's a first step to a lingering death by writer's cramp." He shoved the papers into a portfolio and laid it on the ground. "I have your next . . . ah." He was silent while the soldier laid out four kinds of cheese and poured wine.

"That will be all, Private." He sniffed the wine exuberantly and tasted it. "I suppose rank does have its privileges." Ramos compared this opulence to Colonel McGavin's Earthside quarters. He mumbled something in agreement, but privately noted that rank's privileges varied from army to army.

"I have your next assignment, Ramos. Are you familiar with Clan Cervantes?"

"Only as an area on the map."

The Commandante waggled his head in amazement. "And we visited it together, a two-week hunting trip, not five years ago."

"Can't remember a thing about it."

"Mn. At any rate, we're having a problem with el Cervantes. He appeared to be with the Plan from the beginning, but lately . . . well, the details aren't important."

"He's having doubts?"

"Perhaps worse than that. El Alvarez suspects treachery."

"Does el Cervantes have a conveniently aged son?"

"Unfortunately not. He's an old man; his son is almost fifty."

"But it's a good situation. His only grandson is twelve years old, and there is nobody in the family who can take over in the *Senado* should something happen to his son." He smiled pleasantly. "They have been cursed with daughters."

"Then I am to challenge this fifty-year-old man and kill him."

"Yes. It would be that simple, except for one thing." He leaned back against the tree. "There's a price on your life now, Ramos. In every clan except Alvarez. El Tueme offers ten thousand for your head."

"So first . . . we have to change your head."

"Plastic surgery?" *Once the scalpel touches plasti-flesh . . .*

"Of course. We've discussed the possibility."

"Seems extreme. Could they change me back afterwards?"

"I don't know. I imagine not."

"I don't like it."

Julio shrugged. "It's your head, Ramos. I'd hate to see you lose it out of vanity."

"Let me think . . . do you have a copy of the picture they'll be using to identify me?"

"Yes." He rose. "Come with me." The Commandante led him past two sets of armed guards into the opulent house. He thumbed open the door to a large study.

He opened a heavy wooden filing cabinet—also thumb-locked. "Here."

Ramos studied the picture, a good likeness but evidently taken toward the end of his imprisonment. "No problem. Look." He held the picture next to his face. "I don't have the prison pallor anymore, and in this picture my face was puffy with bruises. If I shave off my moustache and crop my hair close, nobody would recognize me."

Julio looked back and forth between the picture and Ramos. "Probably. I'd be happier if you went ahead with the surgery, though."

"It bothers me, Julio. I mean . . . I have so few solid links with the past as it is. I have the feeling that if I lose my face . . ."

"All right. Fine." Julio took the picture back and refiled it. "Tell you what, I'll have Ami bring you some of that lotion, what do they call it, that woman use to darken their complexion." He locked the drawer and took Ramos by the arm. "No more work tonight. Let's finish that bottle of wine."

Ami was waiting for Ramos when he returned home. She massaged *Sol Instante* into every square inch of his skin, and it did a very convincing job. Ramos considered the maxim that a soldier had best abstain from sex on the eve of a battle, and rejected it.

6

With papers and currency appropriate for a citizen of Clan Amarillo, Ramos had no trouble getting into Cervantes. He didn't want to go directly to Castile Cervantes; instead, he monorailed to a small town a safe distance from the border, then took a coach to an even smaller town, one primitive enough not to have video service on its phones.

It was a lovely little resort town, Lago Tuira, and he rested for a day and a night at the inn there. Then he placed an anonymous call to the castle guard at Castile Cervantes, briefly warning them that a hired assassin was after the younger Cervantes. The teniente he spoke to tried to keep him on the line, but he rang off, shouldered his knapsack, and slipped out of the inn.

Clan Cervantes was the oldest settled part of Selva and the part where mankind had most effectively modified the environment. The jungle around Lago Tuira resembled a garden gone to seed more than a typical Selvan jungle. The largest creatures there were no more dangerous than a Terran bear or large cat, and relatively rare. So Ramos could travel through the early morning dark with little fear of betraying his presence by laser use.

Under cover of darkness, Ramos walked back down the crude corduroy road, slipping into the jungle whenever a vehicle approached. Nobody seemed in any great

125

hurry to get to Lago Tuira, and none of the vehicles had any official markings. They either hadn't had time to trace back his call, or had thought he was a crank and hadn't bothered.

At dawn Ramos got off the road, working along parallel to it behind twenty or thirty meters of jungle. By noon he found a climbable tree, pitched his camouflaged hammock in the lower branches, and slept soundly until dark. Then he walked through the cool night until he reached the town that had the monorail terminal. He waited in the woods outside of town until a couple of hours after sunup, then walked down to the terminal, treated himself to a shower and a change of clothes and a hearty meal, and then caught the morning train to Castile Cervantes.

He had no intentions, of course, of actually trying to maneuver Ricardo Cervantes III into a duel. But he had to make the appearance of setting it up.

Castile Cervantes was the largest city Otto/Ramos had seen on Selva; nearly a quarter-million people. He decided a good starting point would be trying to get some sort of job in the castle itself.

Getting off the train, people had to show their identification to a pair of armed soldiers, who checked their faces against a photograph. When Ramos's turn came, he craned his neck to see the picture; it was the same as the one he had seen in Julio's study.

"Who's that, *amigo?*" he asked one of the soldiers.

The man looked at him coldly. "Just be glad it isn't you."

"How long have they been doing this?" he asked the man in line next to him.

"I don't know," he said. "Come in here two or three times a week; never happened before." Maybe the phone call had worked.

At an employment agency Ramos found out that most jobs in the castle required a security clearance. One that didn't was "Dishwasher, Grade 2."

126

The next day he was in the castle commissary washing pots and pans and keeping his ears open. By afternoon he had learned that Ricardo III wasn't anywhere near Clan Cervantes. The day after the phone call, he had taken his physician's advice and gone on a long vacation; hunting and fishing for the month that remained before the *Senado* was to reconvene.

Whether he had precipitated the man's disappearance or not was immaterial. There was nothing to keep him in Clan Cervantes, so he chewed out the kitchen foreman and stalked away. He took an indirect route, through Clan Amarillo, to Castile Alvarez. He called Julio and the Commandante said to come right over, even though it was late.

Bone-tired, Ramos sagged over to the mansion and met Julio in the garden. He recounted a plausible version of what had happened in Clan Cervantes.

". . . so it looks like we'll have to wait, take care of him next month. It shouldn't be any problem."

Julio had been reserved, silent through the whole report. At this he nodded abruptly and said. "All right. We wait." Rising: "Come with me, Ramos. I have something that ought to interest you, in the study."

He opened the door to the study and ushered Ramos in. At the far end of the room a man sat on a swivel chair, reading, with his back toward them. Julio said, "He's here." The man snapped his book shut; turned and stood, smiling.

It was Ramos Guajana.

"Who is this—imposter?" Otto/Ramos said, drawing his sword. The Commandante laughed, one monosyllable.

"Simply another version of yourself," Guajana said, "with no inconvenient amnesia." His own épée danced fluidly into a *garde* position. "Shall I kill him, Julio?"

"No. El Alvarez will have questions for him . . . you may hurt him, though. With a minimum of bleeding, please. This rug is the very devil to clean."

127

"It's strange," Guajana said, advancing. "Almost like fencing before a mirror. But my reflection has pitiably bad form."

Danger imminent, he was all Otto McGavin. Who hadn't fenced in fifteen years. And was exhausted.

Guajana took the initiative with an attack *en cuatro* and Otto swatted the blade away, advanced with a series of short jabbing thrusts. Guajana parried them easily, laughing, then did a simple cutover and pinked Otto just above the right knee.

Guajana jumped back and held his sword up in ironic salute. *"Primera sangre."*

"I think he's good for a little more," Julio said. "Try for the face."

Got to get inside his blade and use my hands and feet. The wound didn't yet hurt much, but Otto could feel his leg stiffening. Sticky bloodstain creeping toward his ankle.

Guajana came in blade high, *en seis,* relaxed. Otto stepped forward, ducked, felt the blade graze his scalp, delivered a sidekick to Guajana's leading shin, heard it break, dropped the sword and struck the man's throat with bunched fingers (left hand) while seizing his sword-wrist; held the weapon high out of the way (decided this instant to not use the neckbreaker, let him live) and punched him hard just below the sternum,

felt Julio's forearm snake across his throat, dropped the broken Ramos, shifted weight, slid a foot grating down the man's shin to crunch on his instep—breaking Julio's hold on his throat—shifted weight again and spun the heavy man over his shoulder and stepped forward to deliver the final kick and

saw laser pistol glint in Julio's hand and knew he
couldn't kick it out from this distance and
(wondering that he was still alive) stepped
back, raising hands:

"Don't shoot. I'm through."

Otto heard running footsteps outside the study. The

leg wound hurt with a deep ache that he knew meant the large muscle was torn. His hair was matted with drying blood and he had the first intimation of a monumental headache.

With his free hand Julio was feeling for Guajana's pulse. "If you've killed him I will personally castrate you with a dull knife." He said this calmly, without any sign of hyperbole.

"Join your friends." The guard pushed Otto into the cell roughly; his injured leg gave out and he rolled along the damp floor. It smelled of old urine and mildew. One man stood with his back to Otto, staring through the barred window into the lighted yard. On the double bunk was another person, female, crying softly.

"God! Is that you, Eshkol?" She responded by crying louder.

"That's her." Octavio turned and even in the dim light it was obvious how roughly he'd been handled. His face was one puffy bruise, eyes swollen almost shut. His tunic was crusty with black blood.

"What happened? How?"

"How, we don't know. Five or six men broke into the hotel last night, after midnight—"

"What were *you* doing there? I told you—"

"I felt that Rachel needed protection."

"Thanks for trying," Otto said. "Go on."

"They disarmed me and then took Rachel prisoner; forced her to open the door to Guajana's room. He didn't seem to surprised to see them."

"Figures. What then?"

"They bound and gagged us—Rachel and me—and took us down the trail to a helicopter. We were here by dawn."

"And they spent the rest of the day trying to make you talk."

"That's right. But I didn't."

129

"Obviously. You're still alive; they must have further use for you. Did they do the same to her?"

"N-no," she said, quavering. "Tomorrow, they said."

"Tomorrow I'm sure it will be," Otto said brusquely. "They're going to kill you both, anyhow. Me too, most likely."

"How can you be so sure?" Slight overtone of contempt, hardening her voice.

Otto felt anger rising, knew it was a Ramos-reaction, tried to ignore it. Pause: "Think about it, lady."

"It seems to me," Octavio said, "that they would want to take as little chance of angering the Confederación as possible."

Otto shrugged and knew it was too dark for them to see the gesture. "The Confederación has already expressed its interest by sending me. It will be much better for Alvarez if she just disappears—you too—rather than have you sitting around as evidence that they abducted . . . what is to the Confederación the most valuable woman on this planet."

"But what about you—"

"Shut up. There's a recorder somewhere taking down every word we're saying. Don't let them know anything they don't already know . . . least of all, about me."

Octavio went to sit on the bunk with Rachel and Otto took over his place at the window. He idly tested the bars; they were solid.

The door opened with one loud rattle and Otto could see, next to the jailer, the silhouette of a man carrying a laser rifle.

"You're next," he said. "Colonel."

7

They knocked him around a bit and drugged him and then knocked him around some more but Otto, because of his conditioning, could look at it dispassionately. Finally they hurt him so badly that he could do the Zen trick and nothing could hurt him any more. They threatened him with simple death and then imaginative, and to both he only smiled pleasantly.

A tiny voice that he heard only very infrequently—so profound was his conditioning—said, *They really are going to kill you this time; you might live with the right combination of truth and bullshit.*

Another, perhaps the rational, voice said, *Your only chance is to throw in with them.*

Or perhaps the rational one was the voice that said, *They have bound themselves to kill you no matter what you do.*

And the trapped animal inside him said without words: *Do anything to live.*

But all of this debate, rational to venal to visceral, came to nothing. If the next beat of his heart would betray the Confederación, the *thou shalt not* imprinted on every cell of his body would hold that organ still.

The fourth time he fell unconscious they didn't shock him back to wakefulness.

Otto woke up in a white room, in bed. Each arm and leg was individually secured, but only two by jailer's cuffs. His left arm and right leg, as well as two fingers of his right hand, were immobilized in orthopedic tractors; he remembered when the fingers and leg had been broken, but the other must have been while he was unconscious.

His tongue counted seven teeth missing. Four had been extracted with pliers, the balance with a truncheon. Amateurs. He knew at least eleven ways to cause greater pain without leaving any mark. He toyed with the fantasy of demonstrating his skills on the men who had interrogated him. Woozy with anesthetic and fatigue, and having no real reason to stay awake, he carried that fantasy with him into darkness.

When he woke up the second time, a man in a white

131

tunic was withdrawing a hypodermic gun from his arm and in a fraction of a second all the pains came back in one electrifying spasm. He fought it and then bent with it and then was above it; the pain was there but it was only a testimony that he still lived.

"Gul' morzhling dogther," he said, and then adjusted to the indignities inside and around his mouth: "Good morning, doctor."

The man just looked over his head and wrote something down on a clipboard. Then he walked out of Otto's field of view and said, "Go ahead."

Julio Rubirez came in with a chair and sat down at the foot of Otto's bed. "Commandante," Otto said.

Rubirez regarded him for long seconds. "I can't decide whether you are the best-trained soldier I have ever seen or are simply not human."

"I bleed."

"Perhaps the Confederación can make robots that bleed."

"You won't find out from me."

"Not by torture, granted." He stood up and, holding on to the bedrail with clenched fists, leaned closer to Otto. "You present an unusual problem."

"I should hope."

"I've been in conference with el Alvarez. He has the idea that perhaps you can be convinced . . . of the value of the Plan. Perhaps not only tell us what we need to know, but even lend your talents to the execution of the Plan."

"You don't agree."

"Of course not. El Alvarez is intelligent and dedicated but he has never been a soldier; he doesn't know enough about pain. He will not believe what I tell him about the kind of person you must be. He thinks he can reach you."

"He may be right."

Julio smiled wanly. "Name a price."

He thought. "I have been . . . what I am—"

"You can say 'prime operator.' Some things we do know."

"—a prime operator, then, nearly half my life. I've been shot and knifed and burned and, in general, have been treated poorly so many different ways and times that I'll have to admit that in a way you're right. I have no illusions left and few emotions."

Otto smiled and knew how ugly it looked. "But I was really sentimental about my left upper molar; it was the only real tooth I had left. So a deal: if you bring the man here who pried my tooth out and cut his throat in front of me, I might talk business."

"Do you know which one he was?"

"No."

"Very well. Orderly!" A young man jogged over, snapped to attention. "Bring me Tenientes Yerma and Casona. And a sharp knife . . ." He thought. "Detail yourself a squad, and bring them bound."

"Sir." Click, about-face, jog.

"You're serious," Otto said.

"About killing them, yes. As to influencing you, I suspect it will not, but . . . I promised el Alvarez I would try.

"Besides, both of them disgust me. They are *mariposas*, the dear boys. And they enjoy other people's pain too much."

You hate to see that part of yourself reflected, Otto thought. "If you know that I'm a prime operator, then you must know what kind of trouble will follow from killing me."

"It's a calculated risk."

"An easy calculation to make . . . it's an extravagant gesture, killing me; rather like assassinating an ambassador. And you're going to do that, too."

"Probably."

"The very least that will happen is brainwipe for el Alvarez and you and everyone else of high rank. And if you drop one bomb on Grünwelt, you've forfeited the destiny of your whole planet. You know about October."

"It's a myth."

"It is not. I've been there."

"Really." He sat down again, propping his chin on a cupped palm. "Did you find it amusing? Instructive?"

"You might find it instructive. No form of animal life more complex than a cockroach survived. The cockroaches have become very large and aggressive."

"You're saying that the Confederación would be so outraged over our killing a very few people that they would murder an entire planet." He laughed artificially.

"The Confederación doesn't murder." *Oh really?* "They released a virus into October's atmosphere that sterilized every female from fish to mammal."

"So they only murdered the ones who lived long enough to starve."

"They supplied food. As a gesture. Men can live on plants and bugs."

Julio yawned. "I wouldn't mind being sterile. Three children are sufficient."

"Don't be stupid."

He smiled. "Don't be insulting."

They sat silently for a minute. "When do I see el Alvarez?"

"He is very busy. You may see him before you die."

"You have a very primitive sense of theater, Julio."

The orderly returned with six armed men and the two interrogators, their arms tied behind their backs. The two tenientes led the procession, erect but very pale.

The orderly handed Julio a thick-bladed butcher's knife. "Good morning, Bernal. Romulo." He slapped the handle in his palm rhythmically.

One answered weakly; the other opened his mouth and his teeth chattered.

"Which of you pulled this gentleman's teeth? It would please him to see your throat cut."

"I would be satisfied," Otto said, "to see them lose a few teeth themselves."

The one who had spoken earlier said, "We both did, Commandante."

"Hmm." Julio looked thoughtful. "Orderly . . . see if there are pliers in that desk over there."

He returned with a chromed surgical instrument that looked as if it might do the job. "Will this do, Commandante?"

"We can only try. Romulo, you may test the equipment on Bernal." He gestured to the orderly. "Untie him."

The interrogator took the tool and faced his partner, talked to him the way one talks to a child. "Open your mouth, Bernal." And whispering: "Be brave."

Bernal gave one small cry of pain when the first tooth came out. Romulo looked at Rubirez, who nodded, and he bent to take out another.

"Well?" he said to Otto.

"I've displayed my good faith. Now will you answer some questions?"

"You've displayed something. No."

He nodded, blankly. "Orderly. Call the prison compound and tell them I want Señor de Sanchez and Señorita Eshkol."

Bernal was losing his third tooth, not making a sound although tears coursed down his face. Rubirez said, "Oh—Romulo—"

The man looked up and didn't even have time to blink. The butcher knife hit with enough force to cut his neck half through. The soldiers and Otto flinched at the sudden spray of blood. Rubirez snatched the dying man by the hair and jerked him down, then hacked savagely twice, then gave a third studied blow that separated the head from the body. He held it dripping over Otto's bed.

"One more?" There was absolutely no expression on his face; no emotion in his voice.

135

Otto choked back sudden bile. "No. That was an adequate demonstration . . . of . . ."

"My 'primitive sense of theater'?" One of the soldiers ran for the door. "Private Rivera. Come back or you will be punished." The private slowed for a second and ran on. The Commandante returned his gaze to Otto, but didn't say anything. The only sounds were the private's echoing footsteps and a faint rustling sound that Otto knew was the headless body, moving. Bernal fainted.

"You may all leave. Take this garbage with you."

A dead man is much heavier than a live one. It took only one man to carry the unconscious Bernal; four to drag out the body. The orderly carried the dull-staring head to the door, set it outside, and posted himself. He told one of the men carrying the body to come back for the head.

"Now, Colonel. Shall we try to get down to business again?"

"If you think you've impressed me, you're wrong. I've known many ruthless men."

The Commandante moved to the side of Otto's bed and laid the point of the knife against his throat. Blood still dripped from the blade and his right arm was hot crimson from the hand to the elbow.

"I'm getting tired of your *machismo,* Colonel." Otto could move his head but knew it would be useless.

"Really? I'm vastly entertained by yours." The Commandante, livid, jerked the knife away. Having lived to see that expression on Julio's face, Otto knew he would live as long as el Alvarez ordered it.

The orderly escorted Rachel Eshkol and Octavio de Sanchez into the room, then returned to his post at the doorway. Rachel was white-faced but composed; Otto assumed that the head had been removed from the corridor. Both of the prisoners were clad in baggy gray fatigues and had their hands tied behind their backs. Octavio still looked very used, but Rachel hadn't yet been harmed. She gasped when she saw Otto.

"I wanted the two of you to see what we've done to your prime operator," the Commandante said, "so you won't have any illusions about your own diplomatic immunity."

"I haven't doubted for a second that you can kill us," Eshkol said through clenched teeth.

"You are all so full of heroism," Julio said, fingering the edge of the bloody knife. The woman saw it for the first time and stifled a scream. "So little perturbed at the prospect of—"

"What has he been doing to you?" She stared at the blood spattered on Otto's bedclothes.

"Nothing to *him,* young lady," the Commandante said. "He asked for a man's life, and I gave it to him."

"Is that true?" she asked Otto.

"No."

"But it is," said Julio.

"You two could get along very well together," she said bitterly. "You are a matched set."

Julio laughed pleasantly. "Women have no appreciation for politics." He addressed Octavio. "Isn't that right, Teniente?"

Octavio looked at him uncertainly. "This means . . ."

"That's right." He stepped behind the battered man and sawed through his bonds. "The masquerade is over.

"*Te presente,*" he said formally, "Teniente Octavio Madero. He has been a good soldier under my command for over five years."

"Octavio," Rachel said with a falling tone.

"The obvious," said Otto. "That clears up a few things."

"Indeed," the Commandante said. To Eshkol: "Now you have no one. Your colonel is a brutal sadist and your confidante a traitor. We'll allow you a few days to think this over. While we decide what to do with you."

He called the orderly over. "Orderly, this man holds the same rank as you—" indicating Octavio—"but I want you to be his orderly for a week or so. While he recovers from indignities suffered for the good of the Plan."

The Commandante glared at Otto. "And in spite of your ministrations, I have my old orderly back. My trusted Ramos Guajana. His recovery saved you from a most vile death."

Julio dismissed Octavio and the orderly with a wave of his hand. He took Eshkol's shoulder and gently pushed her toward the door.

"After you, my dear."

8

Medicine on Selva was only about a half century out of date; in four days Otto was able to walk with little difficulty and his fingers and arm were knitted. As a sign of his continuing clinical progress, they put him back in jail.

It was a different cell. There was no window and the door was a solid sheet of thick steel that slid silently on hidden bearings. Indirect lighting and freshly stuccoed walls. The only smell was a faint memory of disinfectant; there was a tidy commode in one corner, next to a basin. The double bunk was smooth plastic with fresh linens; Rachel Eshkol lay on the bottom bunk, studying the underside of the top one. She didn't make any sign of noticing as the door slid shut behind Otto and locked with a heavy click.

"Our quarters have improved," he said.

"Have they treated you well?" he said.

"I know you detest me," he said. She continued to stare straight ahead and Otto crossed the room, tested out the water faucets.

"Which one are you?" she asked.

"All Otto McGavin. I haven't been Guajana since they started torturing me. The overlay can't have worn

138

off so soon; it's never happened before, but evidently there's an escape reaction. Since the overlay no longer—"

"If you're that one," she said, still not looking at him, "tell me what was the first thing you did when I turned on the lights in your room at the Vista Hermosa."

He thought. "I checked the swords on the wall."

"All right." She swung slowly to a sitting position and looked directly at him. "Yes, our quarters have improved, and no, they haven't treated me well. And I can't detest you very much any more because there are too many others. Myself. Rubirez. Others."

Otto sat down on the commode and started to say something.

"I hate myself for what I've done to the Confederación and to this beautiful planet and even to you. In my ignorance I betrayed the Confederación and doomed this planet to the fate of October. And brought about your death, I'm sorry." All this in a calm monotone.

"I'm not dead yet." The words sounded false to him.

"Yes, you are. So am I. We walk and talk and yet we are dead and already starting to rot."

She had the helpless, dull look of a mortally injured animal, but there was no mark on her. "What have they done to you?" he asked gently, thinking he knew.

"Really," she said, standing slowly, steadying herself with a hand on the upper bunk, "it's not important." She pulled the drawstring on her trousers and they rustled down her flanks. With surprisingly nimble fingers she undid the snaps of her tunic and shrugged it off, then stepped out of the trousers. There was a little spark of defiance in the way she faced Otto; legs apart, fists clenched at her sides—her body was as perfect in shape and tonus as Otto had imagined it, but from ankles to shoulders was a mottled pattern of violets and blues and browns; hardly a square centimeter of her skin, where it had been covered by clothing, was not bruised. She turned to show Otto that they had done the same

139

on her back and buttocks and the backs of her legs; all except for an exact area over each kidney. They hadn't wanted to kill her.

"Every day. Sometimes three or four times." Her voice cracked and she folded her arms on the upper bunk and buried her face but didn't cry. "Rubirez and that . . . Octavio man or Guajana. Sometimes the jailer or some stranger." Otto crossed and picked up her tunic and tried to drape it over her shoulders, but it wouldn't stay, so one at a time he took her hands and guided them into the sleeves of the tunic. She sat heavily on the bed and winced, then folded her hands in her lap and slumped, staring at the floor. She continued: "They—they put handcuffs on my wrists and my, my ankles—and—" sharp intake of breath.

"Please," Otto said. "Don't talk about it." He stooped and picked up the gray trousers. His cheek came close enough to her that he imagined he felt the delicate heat radiating from her breast. "Put these on." He wanted to be gentle and fatherly to her, she seemed so little and so broken, but his body wasn't cooperating.

"No," she said despondently. She stretched out on the lower bunk, her legs slightly parted and raised. She ran a finger lightly along the inside of her thighs; not in erotic gesture, but the way one keeps touching a persistent pain. "Go ahead. I owe you this much. One more won't make any difference."

"I can't, Rachel." It was the first time he had ever used her first name.

The door slid open and Rachel tried to cover herself with her hands.

"Well, well," said the jailer. "You didn't waste any time." Otto was halfway to him when he saw the pistol and halted. "I'd think you would've had enough of that."

He threw a bundle of white clothing at Otto. "Put on these, both of you. Now." Otto separated the smaller items and gave them to Rachel. She turned her back to the jailer and dressed. Otto stood as close to the jailer as he thought prudent and threw his old tunic and trousers at him as he took them off. The jailer jeered and made some pointed remarks about Otto's anatomy.

The jailer gathered up the gray clothing. "You're going to have visitors soon. Try to behave until then."

They sat on the bed together. Otto almost reached out to pat her hand; didn't. "They've never given me a white outfit before," she said. "Maybe this is the way they dress you for public execution. In a way I hope so." Otto knew that if she were going to be publicly executed, she would be dressed only in her bruises. But their inevitable executions were going to be private affairs.

They sat for what seemed like a long time, neither wanting to talk, lost in private thought. Otto wondered, not for the first time, where along the line he had lost the fear of death; the respect for death. Was it just part of his conditioning? That would seem anti-survival, and prime operators were too valuable to the TBII for them to program out the will to live. Maybe it was simply that familiarity breeds contempt.

With some effort of will he thought back to his youth and childhood, trying to recall some incident, some bit of knowledge or disillusionment that eventually led to the invisible army he had joined; that led to this jungle planet and sharing a white mausoleum with——he analyzed the brittle affection he felt for Rachel Eshkol and knew pretty exactly which part of it was sexual, which part was just the somatic sympathy of one injured body toward another, which was atonement for the way he had acted as Ramos, which was retroactive yearning for other women he had loved or had thought he had loved at one time. And some dark growling part of it was probably the cornered beast's obeying an instinct to take one more chance on the procreative raffle before it was too late (he remembered the first

141

time he had seen the corpse of a man burned to death and his horrified fascination with the corpse's extreme state of sexual excitement; was it an instinctive antepenultimate urging or a simple matter of increased gas pressure in the corpse's circulatory system?—he had always meant to ask someone who would know and now he never would). He remembered a boy named Otto McGavin at temple trying his best to meditate while the acrid incense tried to tickle him into sneezing and what a hell of an Anglo-Buddhist he had turned out to be, killing for a living and facing death with no desire for spiritual preparation beforehand—or was that what he was doing? No. What Otto was doing was the closest thing to panic he could allow himself, in the absence of immediate physical danger.

When he was twenty Otto had entertained a conceit about "dying well." He tried to remember how that felt.

The door slid open and nine people came in, in file. The first was Commandante Rubirez. The next was an old man. Then Ramos Guajana, followed by a squad of six soldiers. Everybody was armed except the old man and one of the soldiers, whom Otto recognized as Private Rivera, the boy who had run from Rubirez's grisly demonstration. Behind a transparent dressing on the side of his head was a fresh stump where his right ear had been.

The old man looked familiar, and Otto remembered who he was just before Rubirez introduced him. Strange that *that* should have faded.

"El Alvarez wants a word with you two." He turned to the old man. "One last time, sir. This man is the most dangerous, desper—"

"Enough, Julio. Just leave me your pistol."

He almost said something but instead handed over the gun. "At least let me handcuff them." The old man nodded. Rubirez handcuffed Otto's right wrist to Rachel's left. Then everybody except el Alvarez filed out and the door clicked shut behind them.

El Alvarez looked around, decided against the indignity of sitting on the toilet, and stood opposite the two, leaning against the wall, the pistol pointed loosely in their direction.

"I asked that this cell be built twenty-some years ago. This is the only cell in the complex that has no cameras and no microphones hidden in it."

"Or had none twenty years ago," Otto said.

He shook his head. "I had a trusted person go over it thoroughly last week."

"You have things to tell us," Rachel asked, "that you don't wish known by your own espionage people?"

El Alvarez didn't answer directly. "How many people on Selva do you think know about the Plan?"

"That would be hard to say," Rachel answered. "Everybody seems to have heard rumors."

He nodded and smiled. "That's part of the Plan itself. Actually, I suppose only one out of a hundred or so Selvans knows there is a truly concrete Plan. Most of them belong to Clan Alvarez or are powerful members of their own clans. We haven't yet made a public statement about the Plan because we don't want to encourage responsible public debate." He paused expectantly, but neither of them said anything.

"I believe your Confederación doesn't think it could possibly work."

"That's—"

"Quiet!" Otto snapped.

"I've read your orders, Colonel," he said wearily. "The ones that were in Ambassador Eshkol's safe. In that regard you have no secrets to protect.

"At any rate, the Confederación is quite right. Oh, we could deliver a few bombs to Grünwelt; we would destroy a few cities and millions of people, perhaps. But I know and you know that war is more than just piracy on a large scale, which is what the Plan distills to. We simply don't have the economic resources, not by a factor of a thousand, to maintain a war with Grünwelt

143

—even if the Confederación were not to intervene. We could start a war, but Grünwelt would finish it at its leisure."

"I don't see why you're telling us all this," Otto said.

"It will become clear."

"One thing that *is* clear—" scorn creeping into Otto's voice— "is that our analysts were right. You're willing to gamble the destiny of an entire planet in some convoluted scheme to get more power."

"No. If I enjoyed the exercise of power I would seek to preserve the status quo. There is no one on this planet more powerful than I am. Except perhaps you two. Which is why I've brought you here, of course."

"You haven't gone out of your way to make us sympathetic," Rachel said, and Otto knew her just well enough to hear the leading edge of hysteria.

He ignored that. "I will need your help," he said, "the Confederación's help. But first I need your understanding." He looked at Rachel. "Not your sympathy."

"The Confederación does not meddle in the internal affairs of its member worlds," said Otto. "Except when those affairs—"

"I know," el Alvarez interrupted. "I may know the Charter even better than you do.

"Briefly: What we call 'the Plan' is only one part of a larger plan. You are also part of it. It was laid out in some detail by my great-grandfather over a century ago. Juan Alvarez II, a political scientist and . . . a visionary. A practical man but a dreamer.

"Selva was colonized by dreamers, you know. Political exiles from Terra who brought a primitive kind of communism with them. It lasted less than three generations. It couldn't survive two crop failures in a row and the efforts of nine strong men—the first clan leaders. To consolidate and maintain their power, their fiefdoms, these nine governed in a brutal, arbitrary way. When their heirs succeeded one at a time, they didn't change methods—in a crude way, this is how the balance of power was maintained.

"Eventually the brutality and capriciousness became institutionalized and, inevitably, I suppose, filtered into the conduct of daily life at every level. Do people routinely settle arguments by dueling on any other planet?"

"I don't think so," Rachel said.

"No," Otto said.

"That's one example. There are others. The sum of it, though, is that our way of life is in almost every respect a healthy millenium behind that of any other culture in the Confederación."

"I quite agree," Otto said sourly.

"And it has a built-in stability through the method of succession." He seemed now to be pleading rather than explaining. "But Juan Alvarez II devised a way to subvert that stability."

"And to implement this, you need help from the Confederación."

"That's right. We—"

"Weapons? Money?" *As if I were in a position to make promises,* Otto thought.

"No . . . well, a little money, maybe. Let me explain. Juan Alvarez II suggested that we need set up only a few initial conditions, not obviously revolutionary changes, in order to slowly shift the base of power away from the clan leaders; eventually transform them into powerless figureheads."

"What could you possibly have to gain by all this?" Rachel asked.

"You would have to be in my position, Señorita, to truly understand. Most Selvans are reasonably content with their lives because they know no better; their educations and the information they receive about other worlds are carefully controlled. I was educated offworld —as part of Juan the Second's plan—and I feel, have always felt, dissatisfied. Every bit as manipulated and

145

. . . helpless as are my subjects. That I am ruled by half a thousand dead men, rather than one live one, makes no difference."

"Very poetic," Otto said. "Specifically. What initial conditions?"

"These will be disguised by our preparations for the hypothetical war. Clan Diaz is building a fleet of Foster-type freighters. We are calling them bombers." Otto vaguely remembered that a Foster drive was a reaction jet, powered by fusion of deuterium. Ancient history. "Unfortunately, they will not be finished in time for this next opposition with Grünwelt—to preserve the element of surprise, we will have to attack when the planets are closest—and there will not be another favorable opposition for five years.

"So for the next five years we will have a fleet of new ships and it will not be unreasonable to suggest we make some money with them. Such commerce as goes on between Selva and her sister planet is almost totally controlled by Grünweltische shipping and tourist firms; we can underbid them and still make a good profit."

"I begin to see," Otto said.

"See what?" Rachel asked.

Alvarez made an animated gesture, forgetting the gun in his hand, Otto ducked instinctively. "This way we will have formed a new social class, interplanetary merchants—who will be the only ones with access to wealth outside of our own closed economic system! Each clan will see the fortune to be made, and none will be able to afford *not* to—"

"Wait, wait," Otto said. "I see something else. The closest thing to a spaceport on this planet is Barra de Alvarez."

"That's right," Alvarez said impatiently.

"So you will be getting first crack at the money; tariffs, docking fees—"

"No, no—that's part of the plan, too. I will be in a

position to encourage interplanetary trade by taking a little—"

"As little as you could and not appear suspicious," Otto said blandly.

"That's correct," he said with flinty pride.

"I'm no sociologist," Otto said, "and when we studied interplanetary economics . . . I don't remember anything one-tenth this bizarre. It's about the shakiest recipe for social reform I've ever heard."

"I know my people."

"And what do you need from the Confederación?"

"Mostly advice. And that they not react too quickly if they hear rumors of war.

"As you say, Colonel, you're not a sociologist, but I'm sure the Confederación has many good people who are. And economists and propagandists and psychodynamicists and . . . whatever. People who could review Juan Alvarez's plan, update it, and insure that it would work."

Otto shook his head. "That sounds contrary to the policy of self-determination."

"Your presence here implies that the policy is flexible, Colonel." He smiled. "Besides, the Plan is home-grown. We would only want the Confederación to help us polish it, as I say."

"El Alvarez," Rachel said, "are you saying that the clan leaders would eventually become dependent on the . . . merchant class, and then be ruled by it? Even though the merchant class would have only economic power?"

"Yes. Again: I know my people."

"Your *people*," she said, her voice starting to shake, "I don't think are subtle enough to respond to that kind of pressure." She pulled the hem of her blouse up a few centimeters, showing the bruises. "Your *people* raped me several times a day and beat me without mercy— just for amusement; no pretense of interrogation. I think

147

you are overrating Selva if you think it will be ready for civilization within the next few hundred years."

"I'm sorry. More, I am outraged. But please try to understand—"

"I think I understand more than either of you do."

"No, I mean . . . you couldn't be protected. Nor you, Colonel. I am surrounded by suspicious men and—"

He was interrupted by the door sliding open. Julio Rubirez walked in, leading the whole entourage, guns ready.

"I didn't summon you," el Alvarez said.

"But you did, sir." Ironic emphasis on the "sir." Julio scraped a place on the wall with his thumbnail; stucco flaked off, revealing a metal microphone plate. "Drop that pistol, whoever you are."

El Alvarez gauged the faces of the men covering him and dropped the gun.

"This man is an imposter," Julio said to the soldiers. "As good a copy of our beloved Alvarez as the man on the bunk is of Teniente Guajana."

Guajana picked up el Alvarez's pistol and handed it to one of the soldiers.

"I promise I will find out what he has done with our leader."

The soldier to whom Guajana had given the pistol was already holding a rifle with both hands. He found it awkward and, not thinking, passed the pistol to the only man in the squad who had a free hand: Private Rivera.

"And as for these two . . ." Julio leered at Otto and Rachel and raised his gun.

Private Rivera slipped the safety off the pistol, held it to the back of the Commandante's head, and fired. His skull exploded with a loud report and his still-smiling body pitched forward.

Otto hit the floor, dragging Rachel after him, and scooped up the Commandante's pistol with his left hand. Guajana had just unholstered his own gun and was about to shoot Private Rivera point-blank when Otto fired and opened up the near side of his likeness from hip to ear.

"Drop it drop it!" Otto yelled and all of the soldiers except Rivera did, the whole thing having happened so fast that they didn't even have their rifles unsafed.

"You too, Private," Otto said quietly.

He had the pistol pointed at Rubirez's body and gave no sign of hearing. Otto took a careful point of aim; his pistol arm just below the elbow. "Drop it."

Rivera let the pistol slip from his fingers and raised his hand to touch the stub of his ear.

"I'm confused," he said. "What happened?"

"The first shots of a war," Otto said. And *sotto voce:* "Maybe the last."

9

Terran Bureau of Investigation and Interference
Memo
Secrecy Class **5**

To: Planning
From: J. Ellis, Ph.D.
Re: Debriefing agent McGavin (S-12, prime), mission SG–1746

Following documents submitted:
1. Debriefing transcript.
2. Agent's written report.
3. "The Juan Alvarez II Plan," by José Alvarez III (described in documents (1) and (2)).
4. Various documents pertaining to leave problem.

It is my opinion that document (3) indicates a follow-up mission. Agent McGavin disagrees; I request that he not be assigned to this mission. An edited copy of this document may be of interest to the appropriate Confederación committee.

Agent McGavin was two weeks late returning from this mission. He claims to have accompanied his local TBII liaison, who suffered a nervous breakdown in the execution of this mission, to a nearby planet for rest and medical care, and submits documents in evidence. He claims further that this period should not be deducated from his annual leave, since he and the liaison were married for that two-week period. This would make his absence deductible from sick leave. Please forward documents (4) to his section leader.

(signed)
John Ellis, Ph.D.

REDUNDANCY
CHECK: AGE 44

Biographical check, please, go:
I was born Otto Jules McGavin on 24 Avril
Skip to age 12, please, go:
That May we went to Angkor Wat to celebrate Wesak, it was so exotic and colorful, and the people were so strange, I knew I couldn't spend the rest of my life
Skip to age 27, please, go:
Two assignments that year, one was very pleasant, investigating Article Three violation on Jaica, turned out to have corrected itself while I was in PO, nothing to do but lie on the beach for three months, but then I had to take on the identity of Lin Su Po, Prime Minister of the Eurasian Hegemony, because he was going to be assassinated, nobody ever could explain how that was TBII business, it seemed like
Skip to age 40, please, go:
Wanted to be on the team that adapted the Alvarez Plan, don't understand how they could screw that up so badly, almost as if they had engineered a planetwide
Skip to age 42, please, go:
Filed a formal complaint that I was getting nothing but shit assignments, plenty of seniority for a desk job, then had a PO breakdown when they tried to put me in a 22-year-old's persona
It didn't do you any lasting harm, did it?
Just to the boy I was in tandem with, I felt him die,

sticky blackness with bright hot sparks burning into his brain, think the monitor died too, I never saw her again, when I got out of the hospital they made me a street beggar and sent me to Corbus, spy on a brothel that supposedly employed aliens, actually bioengineered human females, had to shoot my way out again, so tired of all the killing, the woman could have been changed back, so tired of getting hurt, so

Kiwi.

tired of getting new parts.

Elixir.

Tired of being so many people.

Cloak-and-dagger. Frog.

So tired.

Sleep.

EPISODE:

ALL MY SINS REMEMBERED

Ember: a red star slowly dying.

Carbon, a waste product of the sluggish nuclear furnace that gives Ember its feeble glow, percolates up to the surface of the star, cooling. It turns into merely incandescent vapor as it swirls into the star's dim corona. When conditions are right, the vapor sublimes: lampblack snow falls back onto the star's photosphere, and stays.

The drifts of carbon gather into shoals, shimmering black blotches that grow and touch and merge until the last crimson sliver of light disappears.

Its planets freeze over.

But the furnace inside the star keeps burning, insulated underneath the black shell. Its own heat doubles back and stokes it until it flares—not bright as stars go, but brighter than usual. Enough to vaporize carbon.

So the black sun shines white for a moment, and its corona fluoresces magnificently, fed by the vaporized drifts. But it ebbs quickly: yellow, orange, red . . . to a feeble carmine. Waiting for the black snow.

1

"You are going to suffer for this." He was an impressive-looking man, sharp acquiline features with severe creases and lines, hair and eyebrows tangled mats of white and black wires.

"We'll take our chances." The woman behind the desk had the bland but penetrating expression that's the mark of one particular beast, the psychiatrist. She wore a gray suit cut like a uniform. "Somehow, I don't think you'll want to press charges."

He didn't say anthing.

"Do you want a lawyer?"

He leaned forward in his chair. The guard behind him tensed. "I'm not talking about corporal punishment. It's God's will you've subverted, not just the law of men."

" 'Thou shalt not detain'?" She said. "I missed that one."

"You know what I mean. You've done something to me. I'm not sure what. It was like a long dream."

She nodded. "Two months long." Someone tapped lightly on the door. "We can explain now." She touched a button under her desk; the door buzzed and opened.

Two men entered: another guard and a tall, severe man in priestly robes, an exact duplicate of the prisoner.

He shot up out of his chair. The guard put hands the size of house pets on his shoulders and pushed him back down.

The duplicate looked no less startled. His guard clamped an arm and steered him into the office.

"Frog," the psychiatrist said. "Dagger-and-cloak. Elixir, kiwi."

The man's expression changed subtly. He rubbed his eyes. "Jesus. That was a long one."

"What . . . what devil's work is this?"

The psychiatrist nodded at the duplicate. "You want to explain, Otto?"

He eased himself onto the edge of the desk and fingered the heavy cast-silver crucifix that hung to his sternum. "Well, Reverend. Where to start—"

"Start by telling me who you are."

"That's easy. I am you—Bishop Joshua Immanuel. Once known as Theodore Lindsey Dover."

"No you are not."

"In a real sense, I am. Ouch!" He put his finger to his lips and sucked, then inspected the small cut. "Forgot about that." The long axis of the crucifix was beveled to a razor-keen edge.

"I'm also Otto McGavin, a career agent for a certain bureau of the Confederación. You don't have to know the name of the bureau; you don't *want* to know the name. Among our functions, though, is the enforcement of the Charter's third article. You know what that is."

"I don't concern myself with worldly—"

"You can't lie to me, Father Joshua. Ted. I have all of your memories, all of your personality, laid over my own. You know the article."

Otto's double glared at him.

"It involves the protection of alien cultures: outlawing very specific modes of human interference."

"But not missionary work!"

"No, not if it's legitimate. You know as well as I do what the real ambition of your order is."

He sat back and folded his arms. "So take us to court."

"If that would work, you'd be in court right now."

"Testimony obtained under hypnosis is not—"

"We have other evidence. We didn't pick you up at random. But your order could tie up proceedings for five, ten years. Which might be too late for the S'kang."

"Heathen monsters."

Otto laughed. "Who know something you'd like to know. We keep a close watch on Cinder. A lot of people would like to crack that secret; the Confederación itself is working hard on it. Through archeology, though. Not subversion."

"That's why you've sequestered me. You're afraid the S'kang will accept Jesus as their Lord and Savior—and tell us the secret out of gratitude and lovingkindness. So no profits for the Confederación."

"Very few officials of the Confederación even know our bureau exists. We operate independently of anything but the Charter."

"Independently of the law?"

"In a way."

Father Joshua digested that for a moment. "I wouldn't be afraid to defend my order's work in court. Whatever the S'kang do, they'll do of their own free will. We can—"

"Free will is a slippery concept," the psychiatrist interrupted. "Guard, give the reverend your pistol."

Joshua's guard was the only armed person in the room. He unsnapped his holster and handed the heavy pistol to Joshua.

"Escape," she said.

Joshua held the weapon awkwardly. He looked around the room with an agitated expression.

"Go ahead. No one will lay a finger on you. No one will pursue."

"I . . . can't."

"Of course you can't. For the same reason, you'll never tell anyone what you've learned today. And the cell you'll occupy for the next few months will be a plush suite with no locks, no bars. You are programmed not to escape, not to talk. This has become part of your 'will,' which is no more free than any other mortal's."

"That's brainwipe." Specks of sweat broke out on his brow. "That *is* against the Charter."

"If it were brainwipe, I could tell you to stick your finger in your eye and you would, all the way to the last knuckle. Will you do that, please?"

"It's only teaching," Otto said, "very efficient teaching. The way you're teaching the S'kang about death and resurrection."

"Play with words. You have machines, unholy machines."

160

"If you had the machines, they would be holy, no? And you would have succeeded by now." She nodded at the guard. "Take him away."

Joshua didn't want to give up the pistol. The guard pried it out of his hands and jostled him through the door. The other guard followed them out and the door buzzed shut.

"Good to work with you again, Otto." He murmured something polite. "Getting close to retirement, aren't you?"

"Close. Haven't made up my mind." Prime operators were allowed to retire at forty-five, with full benefits, though few enough actually lived that long.

"Wish I had the option." She slid a large sealed envelope across the desk. "This is four-day ink, some twenty thousand words. Any problem?"

"Guess not." Otto knew the details of his mission as instinctively as he knew how to act in the Father Joshua persona. But both would fade with time; eventually, he'd have to rely on his memory. "Read it before I go?"

"No, you have a private cabin all the way to Altair, on the *Tsiolkovski*. Give you something to do—no women, no booze."

"Yeah, I know. This guy is . . . strange."

"Should be rather dull, compared to your last one." Otto's last mission had almost been his last mission. It had ended with him lying in a fetid jungle, his left lung collapsed by a bone-splinter spear smeared with animal feces.

"Oh yeah."

She leaned back and looked professional. "What's bothering you, Otto? We thought we were doing you a favor with this one."

"You haven't been inside his head."

"Actually, I have. I monitored your overlay, of course."

"It's not the same, Sara. You don't get his intensity."

161

She nodded slightly. "He's . . . I've had thirty-some overlays—"

"Thirty-four."

"—but I've never had one come on this strongly. He wasn't scared or confused or passive in the tank. He tried to absorb *me!*"

"It's happened before; never succeeded. You'd have to reverse the polarity of the whole machine. A human brain doesn't generate that kind of energy."

"I know that and you know that. But he didn't—and he was absolutely confident. Even as he lost control, step by step."

"So he's a fanatic."

"That's not it. He is, yes, in his own way—but I've been fanatics before—you know what it is?"

"Tell me?"

"I've never so thoroughly despised a man in my life. I've been scoundrels, murderers, assassins—this man has never broken a law in his *life*. And yet . . . 'amoral' doesn't come close to describing him. He's simply evil. Evil."

"That's a little strong. I know he's a hypocrite—"

"He doesn't have a molecule of religion in his body, no, but I should talk. He doesn't have any ethics, either; nothing but ambition. Human beings, nonhuman intelligences, we're nothing but pieces in a game to him.

"He's even contemplated genocide—killing off the S'kang just to keep others from succeeding where he's failed. To him the act would have no more moral weight than turning off a light. Being inside his head is like being part of an evil machine."

"Well, you're stuck with him. For eight weeks, anyhow." She sat up. "Frog. Dagger-and-cloak. Elixir. Kiwi." Otto's eyelids drooped and he slumped into semi-consciousness.

"When you awaken, you will be about ten per cent Otto McGavin, and ninety per cent Joshua Immanuel. Your reaction to any normal situation will be consistent with Joshua's personality and knowledge. Only in situations of extreme stress will you have access to your abilities as a prime operator. Kiwi, elixir. Cloak-and-dagger. Frog."

Immanuel/Otto stared at Sara with a disturbing glitter in his eyes. He picked up the envelope and left without a word.

The humans who first explored Cinder happened to be there when Ember was cold, covered with soot. They found a planet with seas and rivers, frozen to glass; ground covered with a frosting of dry ice; vegetation dormant in crystalline hibernation. The only large animals looked like beetles the size of washtubs, crawling across the land at less than a meter a day. For water, the beetles would find a certain kind of bush that had a taproot descending thousands of meters into fossil water. They would gnaw a hole in the plant's base and send a hollow tendril down for moisture. They ate the corpses of small insects, slowly.

Cinder was named and catalogued and forgotten for half a century. Then Ember flared and glowed again, and eventually another exploration team happened by.

Rivers flowed and the seas rocked gently under a small moon's tides. The planet was covered with flowers that nodded in the sweet warm breeze; flowers laid out in precise geometric patterns, tended by creatures who were no longer beetles, who fit no known taxonomic pigeonhole.

They walked on four spidery legs and had three arms, one a simple tentacle, the other two terminating in complicated hands. Their carapaces (which the first explorers had found to be full of puzzling organs) were mostly hollow, and served as voice-boxes. They could make an amazing variety of sounds by scraping and thumping the inside of the shell, and by forcing air through a slitted membrane. They did an eery imitation

163

of human speech—and learned to communicate in a matter of months.

They claimed to be over a million years old (their years were 231.47 Standard days long)—not just as a race, but as individual organisms. During hibernation, they claimed, their bodies were rebuilt, their memories wiped clean; when the sun was reborn, so were they. They could only die by accident, and they were very careful.

As a matter of fact, they could also die by murder or vivisection. A xeno-anatomist arranged a rather gruesome accident; none of the creatures objected to his dissecting the corpse. Their lives were full of ritual, but there was none concerning death.

He found nothing that could possibly serve as an organ of reproduction.

He asked them about that, and had to explain what reproduction was. They wouldn't believe him. He showed them tapes of copulation, pregnancy, and birth. They thought it was amusing: humans wasted so much time and flesh making imperfect copies of themselves. It's so much more effifficient to just slow down every fifty years or so and let your body repair itself.

So which came first, the chicken or God?

They had a creation myth, but it was so complicated that it made *Finnegan's Wake* look like a grocery list. One individual whose "hereditary" position seemed to be that of philosopher (it translated as "keeper of useful sarcasms") said that he didn't understand the myth either. What good would it be if you could understand it?

They asked him where he had learned the myth. Where did anybody learn a myth? You ask the rocks.

It was a decade before that made sense. Investigating the S'kang (their name was a sibilant followed by a hollow clang) was like opening Chinese boxes. They never really lied, but they never answered anything directly. "Asking the rocks" was their form of reading.

Their tentacle could hold on to things, but it was primarily an electrical organ. Outwardly, its main function seemed to be killing insects for food. But it could also be used to record information inside the crystal structure of piezoelectric minerals, which were rather plentiful.

The planet was one huge library. They could read and write by instinct, by racial memory. At least no one could remember having been taught.

The real mystery of Cinder, though, did not come from biology, nor philosophy, nor yet library science—but from astrophysics. The planet was not where it was supposed to be.

A planetary system has to fall into one of eleven well-defined morphologies— characterized by the sizes of the planets and how they're arranged in the system—which are determined by the size and rate of spin of the primordial gas cloud that gave them birth. The seven planets that orbited Ember each fit one of these morphologies quite well—except for Cinder. It should have been twice as far away from its sun.

Was it a twelfth kind of system? Astrophysicists said no, impossible. Eventually someone mentioned it to the S'kang. They said it had gotten too cold. So they'd moved in closer.

The amount of energy required to move a Cinder-sized planet from where it was supposed to be to where it was came to about 10^{34} joules. That's equivalent to the conversion into energy of a hundred million megatons of matter, with one-hundred-percent efficiency— enough energy to run all the planets of the Confederación for a Standard century.

Energy is power; power, money. A great many people would have given a lot to know how the S'kang had done it. Only two concerns had the wherewithal to actively pursue the question; the Confederación and Energia General, the cartel that owned every basic patent on tachyon conversion (as well as a piece of every volt that was generated any other way).

The Confederación had a complicated array of injunctions against E.G., keeping them away from Cinder on the basis of their interpretation of the Charter. The S'kang were very much an endangered species, with only 1,037 individuals and no ability to reproduce. The Confederación was bound to do everything in its power to protect them from exploitation.

In the process of protecting the S'kang, they occasionally did ask how they'd managed to move the planet like that. The straightest answer they got was "Very carefully."

The S'kang were not cosmic jokers, laughing up their se'en sleeves at the poor Earthmen. In fact, they were rather naïve creatures, straightforward in their own way. It's true that you could ask the same question a hundred different times and get a hundred seemingly different answers. But the S'kang concept of "truth" was indirect, malleable, subtle. If you tried to convince them that the universe was run by law and logic, they would listen politely. But to them, cause and effect were evanescent fictions: things happened; explaining them was both interesting and futile; the only really important things were slowing down at the proper time, rebirth, and tending the flowers properly.

Consider the lilies of the field . . .

From human contact, they absorbed a quirky and usually harmless assortment of ideas and things. They wore junk and jewelry. Hated human music but collected recordings of city noises. Loved Hilbert, hated Euclid. Kept gerbils as pets; prized caterpillar hors d'oeuvres. Did crossword puzzles without looking at the definitions.

I am the Resurrection and the Life; he that believeth in me, though he were dead, yet shall he live . . .

Were suckers for a resurrection myth.

166

2

"Your Excellency." A fat young priest helped Otto/ Bishop Immanuel down the last steps of the shuttle ladder; then fell to one knee and kissed his ring. "Bless you, sire."

Otto muttered a return blessing and looked around. They had landed on a runway of gravel. There were no buildings in sight—only brightly colored flowers from horizon to horizon.

He motioned for the man to get up. "No customs inspection—no forms to fill out? A refreshing change."

"There are forms, Excellency, waiting for you at the monastery. But they're mostly filled out, except for signatures."

"Very well." He was only half listening. The flowers weren't random splashes of color, as they had first appeared to be. When the wind was still, they made an orderly progression of color, all the way out to where distance blued them to a monochrome. Ruffled by a breeze, the flowers would present different surfaces to the eye, and the orderliness would dissolve into a pleasant shifting chaos; perhaps an alien kind of order. He had seen tapes, but it was different standing here with the heavy perfume washing over you, the flowers whispering . . .

"Pardon?" The man was saying something.

"The first impression is always hypnotic, sire. The beauty becomes familiar, but never palls."

"Now nature reflects the glory of God," Joshua said automatically.

"Yes, Excellency. We . . . all of us feel particularly blessed to be allowed to follow our ministry here."

"Quite so, indeed." Joshua reminded himself: not all of them are in on it. Otto reminded himself: some of these people thought they were joining a legitimate order; have to sort them out. "Well. Shall we find the monsignor?"

"Right away, sire." He put two fingers in his mouth and emitted a piercing, unpriestly whistle.

The flowers in front of them parted and three S'kang emerged. They walked sideways, stalked eyes bobbing up and down, and talked as they came, a soft chittering. Two of them were wearing saddles; the other, a kind of load-carrier with elastic straps. Their shells were glossy blue-black and their skin was of a pebbly texture, yellow streaked with brown.

They were about the ugliest creatures Otto had ever seen.

"You have the supplicants trained as beasts of burden?" Joshua asked. "We decided against that when I was here last."

"Actually, no, sire. Only one of these is a supplicant, the one with the rosary—hello, Paul."

The creature made a sound that was undeniably "hello." With a cricket accent.

"And none of them is here against his will; none of them is paid. In fact, it was their idea—very strange; not a favor, not a duty. Just something to do." He and Paul lifted Joshua's luggage aboard the load-carrier.

Joshua regarded the unsettling beast he was supposed to ride. "You there, uh, can you speak?"

"Yes, of course," it said.

"Do you have a name?"

"Not one that you can say." It made a noise like a sneeze competing with a broken snare drum. "You may call me whatever you like."

He thought. "Balaam—uh, Balaam's. Is that all right?"

"Ay-firmative. The beast of burden that was given voice by your prime principle. Very appropriate."

Joshua shook his head. "You—you know the First Testament?"

"Better than I do," the other priest said.

168

"In one sense of the word 'know,' yes. No/yes."
Staccato thumping bass that was S'kang laughter. "Also
the Second Testament. Also the Q'ran, Zend-Avesta,
Agama, Tao Te Ching, Riq-Veda, Talmud, Analects,
Eddas, *Science and Health with a Key to the Scrip-
tures*—"

"Wait!" To the young priest: "Who filled him with
this . . . apostasy?"

"Not us, sire, I assure you."

"Goddamn right," Balaam's said. "My archeologist
friends."

"He swears, too," the priest said weakly.

"Why did they teach you these things?" Joshua asked.

"They didn't teach me. They learned my function and
allowed me to use their library."

"Your . . . function?"

" 'Keeper of Useful Sarcasms.' "

Joshua nodded, his lips a thin prim line. He tested
the saddle. "Shall we be going?"

"Ay-firmative. Get your ass on your ass." Thump—
thump.

3

Monsignor Applegate was waiting for them at the
monastery entrance, hands folded on his ample pot. He
kissed Excellency's ring and ushered him into the monastery office. Bolted the door.

Undid his collar. "Good to see you, Josh. Drink?"

"By all means. It was a dusty ride." He took a seat
in the only soft chair in the room, the one behind the
desk.

Applegate filled two brass cups with wine tapped
from a wooden cask.

"Well," he handed one to Joshua, "what news—"

"Things have changed, Henry."

"Naturally. Four years . . . we've made improvements."

"Outside, I mean, not here. Since when did the flowers go all the way down to the strip? Is that for our benefit, or—"

"No, it's that way all over the planet. Past couple of years, they've been planting like crazy."

"Because Ember's going out soon?"

"Sometimes they say that. Sometimes they say other things."

"As expected, I guess. How long have the S'kang been . . . helping out around here—and why unbelievers?"

"Just the past few months. The unbelievers, that is. The supplicants have been working for us since just after you left; they helped build the new wing and the, uh, weatherproof section."

"That's a nice mural." It was an odd mural, actually, along one whole wall. Depicting the stations of the cross, the painter's technique improved steadily from the first to the fourteenth: he had learned by doing.

"One of the S'kang did that. An unbeliever, as a matter of—"

"Has it occurred to you that the unbelievers might be spies?"

Henry lowered himself carefully into one of the hard chairs and set his goblet on the floor. "Spies? For whom?"

"I don't know. For themselves; curiosity. If they find out—"

"None of them is allowed to observe any rituals or partake of any sacraments. You're too suspicious, Josh. They hang around helping the archeologists, too. They're just naturally curious and have time to spare."

"How do you know they don't observe the rituals? How can you tell the supplicants from the others?"

He smiled. "That's easy; they took care of that themselves. You didn't notice the ones you came in with?

The supplicant Paul has his Christian name written on his forehead. Well, what passes for a forehead."

"No, I didn't notice. They do it themselves?"

"Yes—they say it's just a matter of concentration."

Joshua shook his head. "Henry. How do you know they can't undo it at will? Switch around, send in a—"

"Oh no, no. You don't know them like I do, Josh. They have definite personalities. It's easy to tell one from another."

"Let it pass, for the time being. I'll look into it. Any progress?"

"Well, yes. We're getting data, cubes upon cubes of it. Confessions, catechism responses—"

"No real progress, then."

"Not, uh, not in the sense of . . . no. Not until we can get the machine." They needed a large self-directing semantic computer, which meant they needed a great deal of money. "Did *you* make any progress?"

"Some." He took a long drink of wine. "None at the Vatican. Couldn't even get an appointment with a chamberlain."

"As expected."

"Worse. As far as they're concerned, we're apostates. Excommunicated."

"Ex . . . how did that happen?"

"One of your *bugs*," he said evenly, "said a little too much to one of the Confederación scientists. He wrote it up as a humorous article in an archeology journal. *Flexibility of Ritual Among the Priests of Sol III.* It's very amusing."

"Oh. Sweet Jesus."

"Somebody. We had better luck with Nuovo Vaticano."

"Them?"

"We apostates have to stick together."

He stood up and paced to the mural. "I don't know, Josh."

"Precisely. That's why you're not in charge."

171

"You don't have to—"

"We don't have forever, Henry. I'd take support from the devil."

Henry winced. "Please, Joshua."

"Oh, 'please' yourself. Or have you played the role so long you—"

"Forgive me." His soft features stiffened. "I was never as strong in my unbelief as you. Nor as good an actor."

"You do well enough. At any rate. Nuovo Vaticano offered us a grant. With strings, unfortunately."

"I'm sure you made the best arrangement possible. How much?"

"Quarter of a million—*but*," he cut off Henry's exclamation, "it's going to cost us. Externally, the grant is a simple gift, to help our missionary work. I have an ecclesiastical document to that effect. There's no document for the actual agreement: ten per cent of the net profits from any patents that result from our researches here. With a bookkeeper breathing down—"

"You told them?"

"Just enough to get the money."

A light tapping at the door. "Mail, sire." Applegate got the mail and locked the door again.

"Don't worry," Joshua said, "I only had to tell a half dozen. And they're bigger criminals than we are."

"We are *not* criminals." He flipped through the flimsy printouts. "There's ample historic precedent—"

"Spare me, Henry."

"One from Earth, marked 'urgent.'" He broke the seal and scanned it. "Josh, what were you doing at Confederación headquarters?"

"What?" Otto said.

"Bishop Salazar says one of his priests saw you leaving the United Mankind Building, November fifth. That must have been right before you left."

"Yes, I was getting to that." *Careful*. "The Vatican isn't the only outfit that reads archeology journals. I got

172

an invitation to talk to a Dr. Ellis. He's on a watchdog committee that looks for violations of the third article of the Charter."

"You're full of good news today."

"He was friendly; didn't make any direct accusations. But of course they suspect. Is that news?"

"Should we expect trouble?"

"I don't know. Inspectors, maybe; spies. We ought to be very careful around new people. New archeologists as well as novitiates."

"We haven't been having much to do with the archeologists."

"Which is a mistake. They're learning from us, and hurting us with what they learn. At the very least, we ought to pick their brains.

"I'll tell you what. Have the clerk set me up an appointment with whoever's in charge over there—"

"Dr. Jones."

"Good, and I'll take along a small barrel of this wine as a peace offering. One thing's improved in four years, anyhow.

"Also, I'll want to talk with everybody who's . . . aware of the totality of our involvement here. Anyone I don't know?"

"No. Several prospects, but I wanted to wait for your approval."

"Good. Set up a meeting for just after I visit the enemy camp."

"All right." Henry took Joshua's goblet and refilled both. "That quarter million is a blessing. We can use it."

"No, we can't."

"Pardon?"

"It's not enough. I invested it."

Henry's expression passed from sudden anger through exasperation to resignation. He set the goblet down gently on the desk. "Half that would buy us all the machine time we could ever use."

"On somebody else's machine."

"Josh, you aren't an authority on these things. We don't have to buy our own; users have absolute security—"

"I'm not an authority on computers but I am an authority on power. Its use and abuse. If the Confederación wants something badly enough, it will have it. No need for us to make it easy for them."

"You're just as paranoid as ever. If you don't mind my saying so."

"When did I ever mind what you said?"

He sighed and sat down. "That's true. It was a good investment, I trust."

"A very good one. Half interest in a new courtesans' union on Lamarr."

"Lamarr? That's nowhere."

"Used to be. They found out its primary's a tachyon nexus, though. Closest one to Deneb by several decaparsecs. Within a year, there'll be people crawling all over the planet. Looking for things to spend their money on while the ships refuel."

Henry nodded. "Are they any good?"

"Supposedly. I have no direct experience, of course." Joshua hadn't always been a Magdalenist; he claimed that earlier vows bound him to celibacy. Actually, his experience with the courtesans' union was both direct and of a rather impressive variety, considering that he had only been there for a day and a night. "Traveling men and women I talked to recommended it highly."

"Quite so," Henry said with a little smile. His bishop never drank in public, either.

"This Dr. Jones. What kind of a man is he?"

"A female one. Young for her post. I've never really talked to her. I get the impression she doesn't approve of us."

"At least she's not the one who wrote the article. That was by John Avedon."

Henry laughed. "What a coincidence. Her full name is Avedon Jones."

"Oh, Lord. Set it up anyhow."

4

"This isn't too heavy for you, is it?" Joshua strapped the cask on the back of the S'kang's saddle.

"Negatron. The Second Testament says 'Bear ye one another's burdens, and so fulfill the law of Christ.' "

Joshua mumbled something and heaved himself aboard.

"Then three sentences later, it says 'Every man shall bear his own burden.' The geometry of this situation is very confusing."

"You interpret the Word too literally. Are you comfortable, or would you rather have me walk?"

"Negatron. If you walk, I have to keep turning around to look at you." One eyestalk peered over the carapace and sort of blinked; translucent iris membrane. They started down the path with a peculiar rippling gait.

The archeologists' camp had a rough, unfinished look compared to the monastery's comfortable solidity. Dusty off-white tents and domes scattered, seemingly at random, across a large area of packed earth—a sterile anti-oasis in a sea of flowers.

"Do you know which tent belongs to Dr. Jones?" he asked Balaam's.

"Ay-firmative. But she won't be there this time of day. Either at the site or in the office."

"I have an appointment with her. I suppose the office would be best." He checked his watch; they were five minutes early. "No, take me to the site first. I'd like to see what they're doing."

Joshua nodded hello to various people as he headed

toward the middle of the camp. No one seemed surprised at the sight of a priest in vestments riding a huge bug, of course, and they seemed friendly enough though nobody offered conversation. Some smiled when they saw the wine.

The site was a precisely circular hole some three meters deep by ten meters wide. At the bottom of the hole, next to one side, the automatic digger sat and hummed to itself. Otto/Joshua had seen them before. It looked motionless but he knew it was making progress, analyzing the patch of soil it sat on, munching away a few millimeters at a time, crawling forward imperceptibly on a programmed spiral. If it detected something that might be an artifact, it would drop a marker, back away cautiously, and signal its human operator. The bottom of the pit was glass smooth, except for a half dozen small depressions where artifacts had been removed.

"Fascinating, isn't it?" Joshua jumped; he hadn't noticed the woman come up behind him.

"Avedon Jones, Bishop." She stuck out a hand that was surprisingly large for her small frame (and surprisingly clean for an archeologist, Joshua thought) and favored him with a grip that left most of his hand bones intact.

"My pleasure," Joshua said, and it was a pleasure, aside from the throbbing in his hand. Dr. Jones had a severe face, complicated by lines of concentration and fatigue, but both Joshua and Otto, sad to say, were inclined to take the main measure of a woman from the chin down. In that arena, the cells of Dr. Jones's body were arranged with the same elegance and precision as those behind her skull: flawlessly. And hidden by only a practical minimum of clothing.

The bone-crushing handshake was a trick she had learned as an undergraduate. A man's pupils will contract with sudden unexpected pain, then dilate according to both the ambient light intensity and degree of sexual interest. She had had a good deal of practice in this technique—having chosen a profession that was ninety per cent male and required long periods of isolated field work—and she carefully watched the dark eyes of this supposedly celibate man while he stared in turn and tried to get his tongue into gear . . . and took his measure.

She could have his balls on a platter.

Amused, a little bit charitable, she rescued him from his temporary aphasia. "Let's go on down to my tent; it's air-conditioned." She spoke to Balaam's: "Is that you, Prescott?"

"Ay-firmative."

"Thought so. What's the square root of the Talmud?"

"Guilt." Thump.

She laughed. "You're insane. Want to come with us?"

"Rather go to the library." It craned an eyestalk at Joshua. "Where should I put the wine?"

"Prescott?" he said.

"Sure, I have seventeen names. Don't different people call you different names?"

"Well . . ."

"The best name for any given person. 'A good name is better than precious ointment,' Eccle—"

"Stop! Please. Uh, Miss, Doctor, Jones, the wine is a gift from our monastery. Where should it go?"

"Oh, how nice! Take it to the mess tent, Prescott— but first to my place. We'll sample it."

"He's an Immanuel, Dr. Avedon, not a Borgia."

She gave the creature's carapace a playful kick. "Can't be too careful, Prescott."

They walked across the dirt to her tent, Balaam's ambling sideways alongside Dr. Jones. She brought out a graduated cylinder and tapped a liter of the wine, then sent the S'kang on to the mess tent. It remarked that the place was well named.

Inside her tent, a large cube furnished with light-weight field furniture, it was cool and rather dim.

177

Avedon led Joshua to a chair, set the wine and two glasses on a table beside him. "Only be a minute," she said, and stepped behind a translucent screen.

Two scraps of clothing sailed across the room into a basket. "Dust and sweat," she said over the hum of an ultrasonic shower. "Gives me the creepies." Joshua watched the diffuse outline of her body, turning, and considered the possibility that she didn't know what effect she was having on his poor glands, and rejected it.

She turned off the shower and peeked around the barrier. "Say, you don't have a skin taboo, do you?"

"No, I was raised on Terra. Besides, the body is the temple of the . . ." She stepped lightly across the room to a free-standing wardrobe. "Lord," he said, not too reverently.

"It's not too cool in here for you, is it?" She selected a white shift and slipped it over her head.

"No, indeed." Joshua ran a finger under his collar. "Can I serve you some wine?"

"Sure." She attacked her short hair with a brush, peering into a mirror. Gave it up after a few seconds, pulled a chair over, and sat across from Joshua, legs crossed. Picked up a glass:

"To our separate successes, Bishop."

He nodded and sipped. "Separate but not antagonistic, one hopes. Doctor."

"Oh, call me Avedon. Every other creature on this planet does."

"Thank you, Avedon. You may call me Joshua."

"Ambitious name for a religious leader, isn't it? Related to 'Jesus'?"

"Indeed. I was born with it, though. If they'd named me Prescott, I might have become an anthropologist."

She laughed. "Down to business. You came here to pick my brain."

"Well, I wouldn't put it that—"

"Badly? Don't worry, I'll pick your brain, too. We

178

haven't had much contact with your people. I'm curious."

Joshua studied her face and said, "You knew enough about us to write the 'John Avedon' article."

She laughed, a hearty bark. "I wondered if that would get back to you."

"Oh, it did." There was no point in telling her how much damage the article had done. "If it were about some other order, perhaps I'd be more receptive to the humor."

"Well, you have to admit . . ." She took a drink. "Nothing personal, Bishop. But to an outsider, your order seems, um, strange. Not very Catholic."

"I know."

She leaned forward, idly scratching an ankle, a posture calculated to expose. "Celebrating the flesh—I'm surprised the Holy See gave its approval."

"They are not so hidebound." Joshua carefully looked away. "In fairness, though, our tenets were more conservative when they gave their approval. We have evolved over the years."

(In fact, the Congregation of Mary Magdalene had been invented by Joshua twenty-seven years before. He and two accomplices, cynical hedonists all, had mapped out the order's "slow evolution" away from poverty, chastity, and obedience well ahead of time. It had taken eight months and forty light years.)

(Until the TBII had kidnapped Joshua and put him into personality overlay, he had been the only living person who knew the true story of the Magdalenists' maculate conception. The two other "founding fathers" were dead; one of natural causes, the other because he had had the imprudence to be convicted of the forcible rape of a minor on a planet too primitive to have brainwipe.)

"I was told you were under vows of another, stricter order," she said. "I'm a little surprised that you . . . seem so human." She nodded at his glass of wine.

"Not really." Who had she been talking to? "I went to seminary under temporary Trainist vows. I'm no longer bound by them. Except out of habit."

She smiled but resisted the obvious pun.

"Tell me about your work," Joshua said. "Have you learned much about the S'kang?"

"Not much. Only what you can infer from a lack of data." She looked thoughtful, then suddenly tired. "Fourteen other stations like this one, all around the planet. Digging holes.

"They don't use tools; evidently, never *have* used them. Therefore, no permanent artifacts."

"Except the stones they talk to?"

"Negatron." Balaam's must have picked up that annoying mannerism from her. "We've never found one, except on the surface. Prescott says they don't ever get buried."

"That's helpful." He sipped his wine. "No artifacts at all? It looked like the digger had found a few things."

"You know how a digger works?" Raised eyebrow.

"Uh, saw one in a museum. A model."

She nodded. "Well, those were just rocks. We're going to send a few back for the geologists." She got up suddenly, went over to the closet, and rummaged through a box. "Here, this is the best one." She tossed a fist-sized white rock at him.

He managed to catch it without spilling his wine. "Seems rather light."

"Too light." She sat down. "Chemically, it's dolomite. Physically, it's like no rock we have records of. Too porous; its specific gravity is around 2. Dolomite's 2.85.

"We've been finding these at all of the digger stations, all over the planet, the past couple of months. Never found them in higher layers."

"That's interesting."

"You bet it is. But we're just a bunch of archeologists and xeno-anthropologists. Together we know about as much geology and planetology as a bright undergraduate."

"I'd have thought you would bring at least one—"

"That would be logical." She made a face. "Research-funding committees aren't . . . especially when twenty different universities are involved. Nobody could send more than two field people, and nobody wanted to supply the token planetologist."

"I thought you were here on a Confederación grant."

"Partly. They matched funds with the Sagan Consortium, and provided transportation."

"Their interest is not primarily archeological, I take it."

She smiled. "Negatron." Laughed. "Some people will believe anything."

"You don't think that the S'kang actually moved their planet in closer?"

"What do you think?"

"I'm ignorant of science. At any rate, I'm more concerned with their souls than their world." The Otto part of him shuddered inwardly. "Wasn't some sort of consensus published?"

"It sure was—widely published. And I'm glad; otherwise, we'd never have gotten funding. But all it really said was that *most* of the S'kang, *most* of the time, claim that they moved the planet in to improve the weather. Sometimes they say the planet did it by itself; sometimes that they moved it outwards, because it was too warm; sometimes they don't even understand the question.

"Face it. As likable as the creatures are, they're total imcompetents in dealing with physical reality. They can't put two and two together and come up with the same answer twice. They'll hold a screwdriver the wrong way, if it amuses them. And they're mad as hatters.

"Take Prescott: he absorbed all of Roger Bacon in a week—photographically. He could recite page after page. But ask him about the scientific method, and all he can come up with is an outrageous pun. In Latin."

181

"Can you be sure there's not a larger joke involved? That he does really understand it, and is hiding his understanding from you?"

"Why would he do that?"

"I don't know. Just a feeling I have sometimes. You should hear their catechism responses."

She leaned forward. "That might be interesting. In an anthropological sense, I mean."

"Well, we do have cubes . . . of some of them. I wouldn't see any harm in your making copies. Liturgical responses, too; anything but the confession."

"Confessions? How can they sin?"

"They can theoretically break eight of the ten—"

Somebody was scratching on the tent flap. "Avedon. Digger's beeping."

"Oh, hell." She stood up. "Come on in, Theo."

A young man, shirtless, slipped through the flap. He was wearing a small silver cross on a chain around his neck. "Theo Kutcher, Bishop Joshua Immanuel." Kutcher stiffened.

"Good afternoon, brother," Joshua said.

"Good afternoon, sir."

"I'll be back in a few minutes," she said. To Theo: "Don't start any arguments till I get back."

Joshua watched Avedon depart and sat back, hands folded benevolently. "What sort of argument should I expect, Theo?"

Theo sat down in the chair she had vacated and put his feet up on the table between them, rattling the glasses. "Oh, I don't think we really have any basic differences of opinion." He smiled sardonically. "Colonel."

5

"Pardon?" Otto twisted the catch that converted his heavy crucifix to a three-pointed razor on the end of a chain.

Theo raised a hand, palm up, cautioning: "Now don't do anything. I'm one of us."

"And who would we be?" He was just the right distance. Throat or eyes?

"The TBII; I'm a Class 2 operator, Meade Johanssen. You're—"

"I know who I am. PO?"

"No, just forcelearn and identity switch. I've been here since the beginning; too long for P.O."

"They didn't tell me there was another operative on this planet."

"Well . . . that's probably bureaucracy. You're from Charter Violations; I'm routine surveillance."

"You knew I was coming?"

"Yes. They said—"

"You're to write a report on my performance."

"Oh no." *Too fast; liar.* "Just offer assistance if it's needed. And information, since the TBII can contact me more or less directly. That's what I'm here for now —very convenient, your coming over. I would've had a hard time getting you alone, over at the monastery tonight."

"You don't know the half of it." Tonight was the meeting with those "aware of the totality" of the Magdalenists' mission on Cinder.

"I have bad news. The real Joshua Immanuel escaped from Earth the day after you left."

"What? Impossible."

"That's what I would've thought. But he evidently broke the conditioning and just walked out. They assume he had at least six hours' head start . . . six hours before they'd discovered he was gone, the Earth bishop made a massive personal credit transfer from the Magdalenists' account. Seventy-five Kays."

Otto whistled. "They'll never find him. He could get the best body sculptor on Earth for a tenth of that.

"Are they sure he left Earth?"

"They interrogated the bishop. Joshua told him about the PO and substitution—"

"Not smart."

"—and said he was coming here to kill you."

"That's absurd." Otto/Joshua smiled. "Does he think he can sneak up on me?"

"Well, he doesn't have to come in legally." Nobody was allowed on the planet without a Confederación pass. "He has enough money to charter a private yacht. Does he know how to fly?"

"Yes, but only genteel stuff." He drummed fingers on his knee, thinking. "If you or I were doing it, we'd . . . I guess charter a small craft at Epsilon Indii. Time it so we'd come out of nospace on the day side, while this part of the planet was dark. Bring it in low and land sometime before dawn, in a wilderness area—"

"And there aren't any, not within a thousand kilometers."

"Hm. And he'd probably crack up if he tried it. If he even thought of it.

"More likely he's going to come in as a ringer. Are you expecting any—" Footsteps. "Within the overall fellowship of Christ our Lord. You have to understand—"

Avedon came through the flap. "I don't know what's wrong with that machine. Six times in four days—what, you aren't at each other's throats yet? I'd think a Skinner Baptist and a Catholic wouldn't have much to agree on."

Theo stood up. "I've forgiven him his conditioning, and he's forgiven me my parents. Same thing."

"Only God can forgive, brother. But I can understand."

Theo started to leave but Avedon put a hand on his shoulder. "Hold on, Theo. We've got to go take that machine apart, right now.

"Joshua, I'm sorry I have to run. We'd love to see

184

those cubes. And of course you can copy any of our data that look interesting."

"Most gracious of you."

"Want to try again tomorrow, same time?"

"Certainly . . . and Theo, drop by the monastery any time. We can give each other food for thought."

"You won't convert me, you know."

"We aren't here to convert humans." Joshua walked out with them.

"What makes you think that they won't benefit more from the trade than we will?" Applegate was fuming. "There's nothing stopping *them* from renting time on a semantic computer."

Joshua shook his head. "Do I have to do all of your thinking for you? The data we give them will be worse than useless." He picked up a cube and turned it around in his fingers. "The catechism is just question, response; question, response. As often as not, the responses don't make any sense, correct?"

Applegate nodded, his lips a thin line.

"But we assume there is some sense behind their illogic. So subtle or so complicated that an unaided human brain can't see it."

"This is not exactly news to me."

"But no matter what the logic is, we can destroy it. It's simply a matter of—"

"Of course. Randomize the responses. We keep the real cubes and—"

"Right. Mixing in some of the questions where the answers make sense . . . maybe all of those." He nodded at the small gray box in the corner. "Your machine can be set up to do that, can't it? By tomorrow?"

Applegate rubbed his chin. "I suppose. I'll have Sister Caarla help me." He looked at his watch. "She should be here any time."

"Good." Joshua got up and paced, pretending to

study the wall mural. "Say, we don't have any new people coming in soon, do we?"

"Not with the cold period coming on. Why?"

"Just curious." So when the real Joshua arrived, it would be as an archeologist. "We have plenty of people for the work ahead?"

"Too many by a large factor. But the ones not involved do give us protective coloration, I guess."

Two soft knocks. "Come in," Joshua said.

Four women and three men, the rest of the inner circle. The last one locked the door.

"Fine. Let's adjourn to the winter room." At the other end of the office was a windowless steel door. Applegate unlocked it.

It was a warm, bright room full of flowers, about twenty meters square. The illumination duplicated that of Ember at its brightest; heating elements above the frost line would keep the ground warm through the half-century of winter. Not that they expected to wait that long.

There was a row of comfortable chairs along one wall. They all sat except Joshua.

"Caarla," he said, "you're still in charge of selection?"

"Yes. We have it boiled down to five: Matthew, Peter, Heli, Joseph 2, and the one the archeologists call Prescott."

"Prescott? He's an unbeliever."

"Yes, but he's the easiest to communicate with."

The others must be real prizes, Joshua/Otto thought. "How do you propose to lure him in here?"

"He might do it out of curiosity. Or we could wait until he starts to go dormant; carry him in."

"I'd veto that." Brother Judson, the closest they had to an exobiologist. "We don't have any evidence that the process is reversible. Being in the wrong environment might kill him."

"It might kill all of them," Applegate said. "We have

186

to be a little cold-blooded. There's a lot at stake." Nobody knew whether the S'kang change-of-state was triggered by climactic change or by some biological "clock." But one thing was certain: with its vastly slower wintertime metabolic rate, a S'kang couldn't survive for long in a warm, humid environment.

"Yes," Joshua said. "We ought to stick with Caarla's recommendations. Brother Colin?" He was the group's semanticist.

"I've completed my list," he said. "Over three thousand questions, nearly a thousand of them repeated at least once, under some non-Aristotelian transformation. The early ones are catechistic, or even strictly liturgical. They evolve into questions that deal entirely with the creatures' perceptions of the objective universe."

"Well . . ." Joshua began. Someone was pounding on the door in the other room. "I'll get it. Hold until I get back."

He shut the steel door and opened the wooden one a crack. "Yes?"

Brother Desmond. "Sire, you'd better come to the communications room. There's a petitioner in orbit, asking permission to land."

"Without a permit?"

"No, sire, she was issued a permit on Epsilon Indii. She claims to be fleeing religious persecution on Dakon."

He slipped through the door. "I'll speak with her." If it was Joshua, he had just cemented his fate. Complete sex-change surgery, including skeletal modification, takes weeks. Otto knew too much about overlay techniques to be fooled by a superficial job.

The communications room was a rustic stuccoed cell like all of the others, except for the far wall, which was dominated by a large flat screen and a horizontal bank of slide-out modules of electronic gimcrackery.

The old woman's face didn't resemble Joshua's at all, but the shoulders were a fatal giveaway. Otto/Joshua was *in* that body, and he knew where the bones were.

When "she" spoke, Otto was certain. You can shorten or lengthen a person's vocal cords to change the voice's pitch, but you can't do much about sentence rhythm and word choice without repatterning the brain's speech center, which can't be done quickly.

"Brother Desmond was telling me," she said, "that the missionary work is almost complete for another fifty years. This is all right with me. I only want a place where I can spend my last years in peace."

"What was your trouble on Dakon?" Joshua asked.

"They were trying to have me committed—brain-wiped, actually—because they claimed I was teaching antisocial principles to their children. In a private Sunday school.

"Actually, they just wanted to seize my money. I brought it with me." She held up a draft. "Fifty Kays in Confederación pesos. I'll give it to your order in exchange for sanctuary."

Joshua suppressed a smile. How does it feel to bribe yourself? "The money is welcome, or course, but not necessary. We wouldn't refuse a soul in distress."

She was calling from the shuttle station. "Do you have your own flyer?"

"No. I rented one at Epsilon Indii."

"Well, send it back and take the morning shuttle down. I believe it breaks orbit at seven."

They exchanged courtesies and the screen went blank.

"I suppose I should bunk her with Brother Follett," Desmond said. "They seem to be about the same age."

"That sounds all right. And wake me at seven. I'll go down alone to meet her."

"As you wish, sire." Probably thinking unbrotherly thoughts. "I'll have Paul and two others saddled."

"No . . . I think that might not be a good idea. Surely she's never seen a S'kang before. They can be quite a shock if you aren't prepared.

"If she has luggage, we'll send a S'kang back for it. The walk up will give me time to accustom her to the idea." Of course, a S'kang might not even recognize murder, if it were done properly. But no need to take chances.

He already knew how he would do it. It would be absurdly simple.

He went back to the winter room and told the others about this latest development.

"It seems suspicious," Applegate said. He explained to the others: "Bishop Immanuel was questioned by a Confederación official on Earth. He thinks they may suspect us of a Charter violation and send in a spy."

"Tomorrow," Joshua said, "I'll take Desmond with me when I go over to the archeologists—say I need help with the cube transcriptions. While he's gone, Caarla, you get on the subspace and check both Epsilon Indii and Dakon. Try to get a picture of her."

None of which would happen, of course, after the tragic accident.

With the promise of action coming in the morning, Joshua found it hard to concentrate on the routine details of the planning session.

Two new members were proposed: Brother Anzio and Sister Krim. Anzio had a background in computer repair and maintenance—and he seemed to have joined the order under false pretences. Applegate had discovered that he was a felon, having embezzled a small fortune from a credit union on Macrobastia. He was evidently hiding out, waiting for the statute of limitations (ten years for this crime and planet) to make him a free man.

Sister Krim might be equally useful. She was a natural polyglot, knowing a dozen human languages. Though not an academic, she was an enthusiastic amateur scientist, and didn't hide the fact that the main reason she had joined the order was to study the S'kang. Unfortunately, she seemed a little soft-hearted about them.

They decided to go with Anzio and keep Krim under

observation. If the creatures seemed to thrive in their artificially maintained summer, maybe they would let her in on the game—or at least enough of it to take advantage of her experience.

Brother Judson gave Joshua a guided tour of the winter room. It was a pleasant, perfumey place; thousands of flowers transplanted into the same patterns that the S'kang used. Breezes, bugs—if you didn't look up, you might think you were actually outside. The "sky," though, wouldn't fool anybody: sprinkler system and greased track for the artificial sun.

After the meeting, Joshua made sure that Caarla and Applegate could do the answer-switching job. Then he went outside.

No stars. Ten steps away from the monastery, where an outside light marked the door, it was total darkness. The dense, cold mist sucked warmth from his body. In a few days, Ember would black out completely. The flowers would die, snow would fall, the creatures would slow down. All but a few.

Suddenly depressed, Otto went back inside. He went to the kitchen; it was deserted and not warm.

He took a candle to his cell, sat on his bunk, and with slow deliberation assembled a weapon for tomorrow, hid the weapon under clothing, took a pill, and slept.

6

Joshua stood restlessly by the gravel landing strip, watching Ember rise, its dull glow further attenuated by morning mist. It looked like a diseased fruit, red mottled with black and orange.

The flowers rustled behind him in the slight breeze. For the hundredth time he turned around and checked. No one there.

In the folds of his voluminous sleeves, a long-bar-

relled ultraviolet laser. He looked like he was standing
with his hands clasped, contemplating the sky.

He saw the shuttle before he heard it, wingtip lights
flashing red and green.

(The shuttle would land on skis, sliding down two
kilometers of gravel, airscoops reversed for ramjet braking. Its Achilles' heel was the "live" strut that connected
the ski to the fuselage: it contained a rather delicate
real-time thinker that compensated for the bone-grind-
ing vibration. A megawatt burst would scramble it.)

The flight recorder would be a problem. He'd have to
send a message, through "Theo," to make sure Confederación officials on Epsilon Indii would cover it up.
A malfunction in the thinker.

Now it was gliding fast, a couple of meters off the
ground; now it touched down, sweeping toward him,
continuous loud scrape of metal against gravel, roar of
the ramjets' suck and whine.

Two-handed grip on the laser, deep-breath-let-half-
out, good image through the fat scope, hold fire until
it's even with you. If Joshua was sitting on the right
side of the shuttle, the last thing he would see would be
his black-robed double killing him.

Fire. Track and fire again. The snap-snap-snap of the
laser lost in the thunder of the massive craft's braking.
Live strut gives way: ski squirts out behind. Wing dips
and catches the ground.

The shuttle spun twice and then leaped cartwheeling
into the air. It hit nose-first and disintegrated with a
rending crash, hundreds of separate pieces, large and
small, skittering along the gravel, continuing to break
up.

Otto/Joshua dropped the laser into the trench he had
prepared at the edge of the strip and kicked dirt and
gravel over it. Then he ran toward the disaster he had
manufactured.

The main part of Joshua's body lay at the end of a
ten-meter smear of blood and fragments. Otto toed it

191

partway over and was relieved to see the pristine translucence of plastiflesh shredded among the more mortal remains.

He tongued a pill that was a selective vasoconstrictor. It made his face pale, hands clammy. Approximating a normal human reaction.

He turned around and, in the flowers, saw the blueblack sheen of a S'kang carapace. In an instance, it was gone. A trick of Ember's strange light on the shifting flowers? Not likely.

He walked to the edge of the flowers and saw no evidence. But that didn't mean anything; the creatures moved through the beds like snakes through grass.

No matter. It wasn't likely that the S'kang had seen the whole affair, and even if it had, it wouldn't understand. He found the pathway to the monastery and, discomposing himself, began to run.

"It was terrible. Simply terrible." Joshua accepted a cup of chicory from Avedon, spilling a little as his hand trembled.

Avedon put a hand on his knee. "These things happen. I'm sorry that you had to witness it."

He nodded, staring into the cup. "At least there must have been no pain . . . the Lord moves in mysterious ways. All we really know about her is that she was miserable—hounded, betrayed, discredited on her own world. Perhaps it was for the best."

"I could never accept that. Any kind of life is better than death."

"I'm afraid I agree with you. Though it's a confession of a weakness in my faith." He took a sip of the chicory and set the cup down. Opened the pressboard box he'd carried in with him.

"Well. These are the cubes we talked about."

She accepted the box and thanked him, tacitly agreeing to change the subject. "Give us something to do after Ember goes out."

"You're all staying on?"

"No, just four of us." A few heavy drops of rain thumped on the tent's roof; she got up and crossed to peer through the flap. "After the last S'kang goes dormant, most of the crew's leaving. Plenty of work these next couple of weeks, observing the S'kang as they go through their metabolic change. After that, just maintenance and analyzing old data."

"For fifty years?"

She shrugged. "For as long as the Sagan group and the Confederación keep funding us. I'll be here for a year, with Theo and two others. Then another team comes in to replace us. What about you?"

"I'll stay for a while. No really pressing reason to leave, and I want to see the winter. It's a relief to be away from the pressures on Earth, and I trust the man I left in charge."

"That's a healthy attitude . . . I'm going to hate like hell giving up the reins, no matter who it is." The tempo of the rain suddenly increased, an irregular rattling. "You're on foot?"

"Yes." Joshua stood. "Suppose I'd better start back."

"Before you have to swim. Let me get you a hat." She found a bright orange plastic safety cap. He eyed it warmly. "Go on, take it. It's better than nothing."

"I suppose." It was a few sizes too large; sat on his head like a garish salad bowl.

She laughed. "It'll keep your ears dry." She led him to the flap, her hand lightly on his bicep. "Thanks for the cubes, Joshua. Come over any time you want to copy ours."

"Well, that's really out of my sphere." He looked through the flap; still just sprinkling. "I'd meant to bring Brother Desmond, but he was too upset by the . . . funeral."

"Understand." She patted his arm. "We'll be in winter quarters by the next time you come over. Ugly brown building by the digger site, you can't miss it."

"All right." Joshua pulled his collar up and stepped out into the light rain. Once out of sight, he put the ridiculous hat under his arm.

The ground was still fairly dry, raindrops making small craters in the dust. But the sky was dark gray, with low black clouds sliding in from the east. He walked faster.

As he neared the edge of the flowers, a S'kang spider-walked over to join him. "Bad afternoon, Father Joshua."

"It is that. Balaam's?"

"Ay-firmative. You have been with Dr. Avedon?"

"Yes."

"Alone?"

"Yes."

"Are you in love with her? Are you going to mate?"

Joshua kept a straight face. "I don't think so. Why do you ask?"

"I don't know. It's a mystery."

They walked along in silence. The rain increased suddenly, spattering flowers. Joshua put the hat back on and listened to the drumming.

"Did you tell her about killing that new one?"

Otto: "What do you mean?"

"I saw you point that thing at the spaceship and make it crash."

"No, uh, that was a . . . kind of crucifix, for travelers. I was blessing it, the landing."

"Didn't work, though."

Joshua sighed. "No. Sometimes blessings don't work, prayers aren't answered."

"Many human things don't work. I don't know why you allow it."

He gave a noncommittal grunt.

"Why did you want a crucifix that works like a laser?"

Otto flinched. "It's difficult to explain." Have to get rid of him. "Balaam's, would you do me a favor?"

194

"If I can understand what you want; if there's time before I slow down."

"Well, that's just it. It's important to me that you be somewhere else when you slow down. Not near the monastery. In fact, I would like it if you left now."

"Are you afraid that I'll tell someone you sinned?"

"Not really—well, yes. My sinning is a matter of interest only to me and to my confessor."

"Not to God." He thumped, laughing. "I was leaving soon, anyhow. There is very little food when it gets cold; each one has his own area to search in. I could leave now." He stopped walking. "Besides, if I understand what you are not saying, you will kill me too, if I stay."

Otto didn't say anything.

"I appreciate having the choice. I know how important this would be to a human." He held up a tentacle. "Goodbye, Joshua."

Otto watched him disappear into the flowers. *Getting soft in your old age, McGavin.*

7

In the course of a week the rain changed to sleet, then snow; the wind rose to a screaming gale, slowed, then stilled; noontime dimmed from rosy paleness to utter dark. The temperature dropped a little less every day, but still dropped.

Otto had sent five coded messages through Theo. There was evidence in abundance: he wanted to close this case and move on to someplace warm. And push papers until he retired, preferably.

It was warm and bright inside the archeologists' kitchen. Avedon cleared the dishes and sat down.

"It looks like we may have a change in plans," she said.

"Really?" Joshua was distracted and rather impatient to get away. Before dinner he'd palmed a new message to Theo and gotten a slip of paper in return. He'd glanced at the coded numbers and could tell it was one word, ending in E. Maybe "terminate"?

"The Sagan Consortium has petitioned to allow us to experiment on a dormant S'kang, try to bring it back to activity. So we can continue our investigations."

"You don't seem happy about it."

"Well, I'm not. The consensus is that trying to bring one back will kill it. Even if it lives through the process, losing that half century of rebuilding . . . it would probably become mortal, and die." She crushed a crumb off the table. "There's a new sin for you."

"Murdering an immortal?" Theo said. "It happened once before."

"Weren't you telling me that was against the law?" Joshua said. "Against the Charter?"

"Which is why they're petitioning. The Confederación is pretty anxious to uncover the S'kang 'secret.' I think they'll bend the Charter to save a fifty-year delay."

"What can you do about it?"

"Quit." She shook her head. "I don't know. If it happens, I guess I'll find out then."

"You don't have a very scientific attitude about them."

"Maybe not. I like them; I miss Prescott. Charter or no Charter, they aren't laboratory animals, they . . ."

She looked at Theo and then Joshua, smiling slightly. "Put this in your catechism. What is neither born nor dies, whose motives and actions are incomprehensible to humans?"

"That's blasphemy," Joshua said mildly.

"Not on my part. I just asked a question." She stood

up. "Will you boys excuse me? I'm tired and it's a long day tomorrow."

The dry snow squealed under his boots. The stars were bright enough that he could follow the path without a flashlight. He breathed hot air through an electric mask but his eyes watered with the cold; frozen tears on his lashes and cheeks.

He was tempted to take the message out and try to decode it as he walked along. But it would be easier with a pencil; besides, he'd lose a lot of body heat, unzipping at forty below.

What would happen if the Confederación approved thawing out one of the little bastards? It would weaken their case against the Magdalenists.

At least he'd killed Joshua Immanuel. One less.

He followed the path up to the light over the monastery door. They'd arranged a crude airlock, plastic draped over a metal frame. He picked his way through the slitted baffles and slammed the heavy door behind him.

He had just gotten out of his boots—the antechamber floor was cold—when Brother Desmond came around the corner.

"Sire, Monsignor Applegate wanted to see you as soon as you came in."

"Tell him I'll be ten minutes or so."

Dressed, he went to his cell and latched the door. The message said: 521 592023 6929298865.

It only took a couple of minutes; he didn't need all of the letters. CONTINUE.

He rolled the message into a tiny ball and threw it across the room. Then the caution that had kept him alive long enough to retire exerted itself. He searched on hands and knees until he found the slip, and flushed it away.

Continue? He was just wasting time here, and his PO would start to fade in a few weeks. Bureaucrats. The hell with it. He let himself slip back into the Joshua persona, with some relief, and went to meet his second-in-command.

Applegate was sitting at the computer output screen. He turned it off and greeted Joshua.

"Find the leak yet?" Joshua asked. The winter room had been leaking heat. The ersatz Ember was supposed to keep it at summertime temperatures, but it wasn't doing the job. They'd had to pump in air from the central heating system, and still the flowers were doing poorly.

"No. Brother Judson's still working on it. He thinks we made a mistake in calculating either the conductivity of the support girders or the permeability of the walls."

Joshua shook his head. "Well, that's not my territory. What did you want me for?"

"Brother Colin had a bright idea." Applegate leaned back in the chair, which complained. "He was disappointed because the S'kang that adopted you, Prescott, Balaam's, whatever . . . disappeared before we could shanghai it. It was easier to communicate with than the others. Colin asked the others where it would be; turns out its territory was just down by the landing strip. He and Sister Caarla went down and fetched it back."

"After he . . . it was already dormant?"

"Yes. It seems to be recovering. It's a little confused, but talking."

"Interesting."

"Brother Judson had a fit. He's too soft on them; came within a hair of quitting." Applegate sat back up and rattled the keys on the console. "Josh, what would we do if that happened? We couldn't allow him to . . ."

"I know," Joshua said after a pause. "If it happens, just leave it to me. I'll think of something."

"I'm sure." Without looking at him, Applegate said, "Balaam's said the strangest thing. Delirious, I guess. It said you—"

"Killed that woman?" Otto supplied.

Applegate looked up, startled. "Yes."

"Said the same thing to me, last week. Wonder what it's been reading over at the archeologists'."

He chuckled nervously. "Thrillers, maybe. Mysteries."

"Or the Bible. Full of bloody murder."

"Joshua . . ."

"Did it say how I managed to make the shuttle crash?"

"Uh, a laser."

Otto laughed and shook his head. "That's a max. Have you searched my cell?"

He hesitated just a moment too long. "Come on, Josh."

"Kidding." *So he didn't find anything.* "Suppose I ought to go talk to the creature."

"Go ahead. It's night in there, but I think the moon's up."

Joshua went through the steel door and waited for his eyes to become accustomed to the darkness. The room's "moon" was the pseudo-Ember, turned down.

It did feel about ten degrees colder than a summer night should. He could hear air rushing out of the central heating duct.

"Balaam's?"

He heard a shuffling off to his right—there. The S'kang was trying to hide behind a tall stand of flowers.

"I won't hurt you." He walked toward the creature. The others were huddled in a far corner, resting or talking. They never really slept.

"They brought me here." No emotion in its sandpapery voice. "I did as you said."

"I know, Balaam's; you did well." *To kill a S'kang, visualize an equilateral triangle, pointing down, with its eyes at two vertices: strike one hard blow at the imaginary point where its nose should be. This will knock it out. Apply thumb pressure to that point for a few minutes, and it will die.* "It wasn't your fault." Close enough now for a savate kick. The charge tentacle undulating in front of its face: supplication? defense? No matter, ten thousand volts with negligible amperage; enough to kill a bug or write on a rock, not enough to hurt a man.

"'Balaam said unto the ass,'" Balaam's quoted, backing away, "'"Because thou hast mocked me, I would there were a sword in mine hand, for now I would kill thee."'"

"Don't be ridiculous." Joshua followed the S'kang. "This isn't the Bible. If I wanted to kill you, I've had dozens of opportunities."

"Human logic, bullshit."

Joshua/Otto suppressed a laugh and sat down. "Balaam's," he whispered, "come here. I have a secret."

The creature stopped. "What?"

"I am not who you think I am."

"How do you know who I think you are?"

"Come on, now, this is no time for riddles. Do you know what the Magdalenists are trying to do?"

The S'kang shuffled nervously in place; didn't come any closer. "It's a mystery. You say you are making my friends Catholics, but you never tell them anything any more. You just ask questions. And now you ask me the same questions, even though you know I don't find them useful."

"They aren't here to convert you at all."

"They, Joshua?"

"I am not Father Joshua. Father Joshua is an evil man. I was sent in place of him, to keep the Magdalenists from harming you, trying to find out the secret of how you moved this planet."

"There is no secret."

"I know. That's—"

"You could do it too."

He sighed. "I'm not interested. I just want to keep them from harming you."

"You're too late. What should I call you, if you aren't Joshua?"

"You can keep calling me Joshua. What do you mean, too late?"

"Perhaps not for my friends. Too late for me. My body tries to go both ways, and my mind, too. If I went outside I would freeze to death. If I stay awake, I will . . . it's hard to find words. Overload. Go insane. Die of old age. Nothing human corresponds exactly. It will kill me, though: I was one, then I was the other, and now I am neither."

"I'm sorry."

"I believe you. Who do you represent?"

"What?"

"Who do you represent? Who is so interested in our welfare?"

"The Confederación. You know what that is."

"Of course." He moved closer. "This is strange. I find you easier to understand. It must be the dying that does it." He made a chittering sound. "I'm getting more like a human. In a sad way. Have you always known you were going to die?"

"I suppose so. Since I was a boy."

"Before that, did you worry about sin and repentance? God, and heaven, and hell?"

"No, I guess not. Because I couldn't—"

"And so you treat us like children. Because we don't reflect your anxieties."

"I think there's more to it than that."

"Please leave. I have something to do."

"Balaam's! How long do you have?"

No answer. "Listen to me," he whispered fiercely. "When Brother Colin asks you questions, don't answer him too directly. If he learns anything, he may use it to hurt your friends." The creature remained silent.

He went back through the steel door. Applegate looked up from the computer.

"Does it still think you did it?"

"Hard to say. Not making much sense. At first it ran away from me, but then it talked for a while."

He nodded. "You ought to take the recorder in with you. Every bit of data helps."

"I'll do that. See you in the morning."

Joshua went back to his cell and confirmed that it had been searched, not too professionally. He'd left his suitcase in the closet, unlocked, full of mufti. They'd looked through it but missed the false bottom. Not that he'd need the penlaser or knockout gas or the dozen other lightweight, miniaturized tools. Not with this crowd. All he needed was the word from his superiors.

He set his mental alarm for 3 A.M., meditated for a few minutes, and slept.

Once inside the office, he took off the quiet slippers and got into heavy socks and boots. No telling how far the temperature had dropped. He knew where the alarm for the steel door was; opened the drawer and clicked it off.

He opened the steel door and thought of a word he'd read but never used: gelid. It seemed almost as cold as outdoors. He stuffed his hands in his pockets and breathed carefully. The air made his teeth hurt. He closed the door silently.

"Balaam's?"

"Over here." The S'kang was huddled in a corner to Joshua's left. He picked his way across rows of wilted flowers.

"I wanted to talk to you. This is the only safe time."

"So talk."

"Well . . . why did you shut up on me, earlier?"

"I was helping my friends. Trying to help. It didn't work, damn it. I'm too awake."

"What were you helping with?"

"Cooling off this place. Also moving the planet closer in."

"Wait. One thing at a time."

"It is one thing." He made an eery imitation of a human sigh.

Joshua waited for him to continue. "Balaam's, I can't stand this cold for very long. What you mean . . . you claim you actually do move the planet closer to Ember? It's not a joke?"

"It's not a joke. I told you. It's very simple."

"You said we could do it too."

"You said you weren't interested."

"I am now." Long silence. "Come on. Balaam's. How do you do it?"

"I'm not sure."

"What you mean is you don't want to tell me."

"What I *mean*, jerk, is that you could do it our way, but you won't. You'd complicate it, make it too expensive."

"I'm listening."

"Let me put it this way. You know that matter and energy are the same sort of thing, really."

"Okay."

"And there are some kinds of matter that *want* to be energy, like uranium."

"So far so good."

"All we do is take other kinds of matter and make *them* want to be energy. We make the energy go in a certain direction. That speeds up the planet and makes it want to go in closer."

"That's all there is to it."

"Ay-firmative."

"You use your *minds* to—"

"Meganegatron. You never will get it. Jerks, all of you. Stupid jerks."

"If we never will 'get it,' what do you mean by saying we could do it?"

"*See?* You see? I told you how to do it and now you ask me how to do it."

"I'm a jerk, then. Please elaborate."

"What I mean is you wouldn't do it directly. You'd use technology: set up big reaction engines and shovel mass into them. You can convert mass into energy with about seven-percent efficiency. Use up half the God-damn planet, keeping it warm. Blow the atmosphere away, too. That's *your* way. Jerks."

"The way you do it is more efficient? A hundred—"

"There you go again. If you add two numbers and come up with the wrong answer, what per cent efficiency is that?" He had been dancing nervously, agitated. Suddenly he stopped. "Did you hear something?"

"No . . . what does moving the planet in have to do with—" Suddenly the moon came up to daytime brilliance, dazzling him.

Applegate stood in the door, dressed for the cold, a pocket laser pointed at Otto.

"Joshua. I think it's time we talked."

Otto shaded his eyes. "Henry?" Ten or eleven meters. The crucifix was an accurate throwing weapon, but he'd have plenty of time to dodge it. "What's going on?"

"That's what I'd like to know. You've been recorded, earlier this evening and just now. You have some things to explain."

"Now, Henry . . ." Otto was playing for time, hoping the man would come closer. In an effort to seem casual, he leaned against the wall.

The wall collapsed as if it were made of sand, exposing the steelite pillars that supported the roof. As he struggled to keep his balance, falling, Otto saw that the steelite was eaten through with some kind of corrosion. He toppled off the raised foundation, felt the stinging cold on his face and hands, and landed on his head, on something hard.

Otto was lying on his back, his face wet. He wiped water from his eyes and saw the office ceiling, blurred. Sitting up doubled the intensity of the pounding in his head.

Applegate's voice came from somewhere. "Now, let's—"

"Yeah, yeah." Otto staggered across the room to the

water cooler. He took a bottle of APQ's from the drawer underneath it and shook out a double dose. Took them, counted to ten with his eyes closed, turned to face Applegate, and tried to sound authoritative while his eyes focused: "I'd call this insubordination, Henry. Gross insubordination."

"Would you, now." Applegate had the laser trained on him, sitting behind the desk, leaning forward, tense.

Otto walked toward him, picking up a chair on the way. He sat across the desk from him, close enough to reach the pistol. "Please put that away, Henry. It might go off."

"You told that creature you worked for the Confederación. What did you mean by that?"

"What do you think I meant?"

"I happen to know that you don't."

"Yeah, that's right. I'm a spy for the Holy See." Otto put an elbow on the desk and tried to look casual, leaning forward. "How do you know that I don't?"

"I checked. You see, I *do* work for the Confederación."

"My God." Otto buried his face in his hands. Surrounded by allies. "What department? TBII?"

Applegate gave him a strange look and laughed. "There's no such thing; it's just a myth to keep the Diplomatic Corps in line. Where did you hear about it?"

Otto grunted. "I get around." That rumor had been old when he was a trainee. Nobody in the DC was fooled by it. "Are you a diplomatic . . . person?"

"No. I work for the Bureau of Energy Research and Development."

"You're a spy for the Bird?"

"No, I'm a research monitor."

"A monitor with a gun. Why did they give you a gun?"

"They didn't; I brought it myself."

"Very resourceful."

"Because I thought you were dangerous, from your

dosier. For years I felt foolish; now, I'm not so sure. Did you kill that woman?"

He stared at Applegate. Beads of sweat on the man's forehead. "I think the winter's getting to you, Henry. Why don't you go lie down somewhere?"

"Did you?"

"Let me show you something." He held the crucifix up to his face and sliced off a piece of cheek. Plastiflesh, it didn't bleed. He tossed it on the desk in front of Applegate.

"Listen carefully because I'm not going to repeat myself. I'm not Joshua Immanuel; Joshua is dead. I'm an agent for a bureau that doesn't exist, made up to look like him, trained to act like him. And if you don't put that gun away, you're going to be in deep, deep shit."

Applegate shook his head slowly; looked at the piece of plastic; looked at Otto. His gun hand trembled.

"Keep listening. Now you know something you shouldn't; the memory of this conversation will have to be destroyed. That's a delicate and expensive process. It's easier just to brainwipe and start over with a stock personality. If you put that gun away I'll ask that you be spared."

"Joshua's dead."

"Oh, hell." Otto slapped his right hand on the desk, hard. When Applegate jerked his head toward the sound, he swept his left hand across the desk and knocked the gun away. Applegate half rose; he pushed him back into the chair. Picked up the gun and put it in his pocket.

Applegate was cradling his right hand with his left, eyes squeezed shut with pain. "You broke my thumb."

"Sorry. I hope not." Otto crossed the room and drew two cups of wine. "If you really intend to shoot somebody, you should put your finger inside the trigger guard." He got the APQ's from the drawer and brought them over.

"If I'd wanted to hurt you, I would've. Take these."

He washed two of the tablets. "It really . . . you really are from the TBП?"

"Yes. Will you answer some questions?"

He sat upright. "You've got the gun."

"Please." Otto sighed. "I've had a lifetime of this. We both work for the same people. I'm curious about what you've been doing. Can't we just be two colleagues and talk?"

He stared at his thumb. "Do you have any identification?"

"No, do you? I think it's just sprained."

"It's turning blue. No, I don't either. I really ought to clear it with my superior before I answer anything." He looked at his watch. "I wonder what time it is in New York."

"Add six hours and 32 minutes. What, you want to wake up Brother Desmond and have him place a call?"

"I could. He's with BERD, too."

"Jesus. Who else?"

"Only Sister Caarla, as far as I know."

"Anybody from the Bureau of Standards? Agriculture?"

"No . . . why should there be?"

"Never mind. Look, if you drag your superior into this, he'll have to go through memory modification too. And everybody he tells. Don't make trouble for everybody."

"I suppose you're right." He touched the thumb and grimaced. "Could we get some ice for this?"

"Sure. Let's move into the kitchen." He picked up both cups and led the way to the door; worked the latch with his little finger.

Applegate walked behind him, studying his thumb morosely. Suddenly he looked up. "Wait!"

Otto turned as he was opening the door, and out of the corner of his eye saw that someone was standing in the corridor.

Sister Caarla, white-faced, holding a pistol with both hands. When Applegate yelled, she fired, point-blank.

Otto's "Hey!" was drowned out by the loud *snap*. Hot sting in his chest. He threw both cups of wine at her, in reflex; thrust his right hand in the pocket, slide the safety off, saw that she wasn't going to fire any more. She'd dropped the gun and was trying to cram her fist into her mouth.

He looked down at his robe and saw the ugly spatter of blood on his chest. When he breathed, it gurgled and foamed. Two sucking chest wounds in one year, some kind of record. He leaned against the door jamb. Applegate grabbed his elbow and held him up. "I'm sorry— in all the excitement I forgot."

"Oh, that's all right." He felt light-headed, detached. "Let me sit down." He coughed politely into his hand; wiped a bright smear on his robe.

"Do—do you want me to give you last rites?"

"I'm not Catholic." Otto started to laugh and stopped abruptly, coughing. "Why don't you get me a doctor instead? Someone who knows how to work the doctor machine?"

Applegate ran down the hall. Sister Caarla was crying. "I didn't mean to, I couldn't hear through the door, you surprised me, he said you might be dangerous—"

"Christ and Buddha," Otto mumbled. "Will you please shut up?"

8

Asleep, awake, he remembered a few things:

Trying to tell Caarla not to let him lie down.

Falling over and choking.

Waking up with the doctor machine sealed over his thorax; Applegate and Desmond arguing about something.

A S'kang hovering over his face. A wall caving in, then reassembling itself, then caving in again.

Fuzzy image of the infirmary cell, rippling, turning hard-edged.

Applegate: "Are you awake, Joshua?"

Otto coughed and shook his head. The Joshua persona was gone; he was Otto McGavin, encased in alien plastic, a dull ache in his chest. "I guess so."

"How do you feel?"

"I don't know yet. All right. It was a new lung, good thing she missed my heart." Coughing spasm.

"Caarla was hysterical. We had to give her a sedative." Otto stopped coughing but didn't say anything. "Will she be in trouble?"

After a while he answered. "No. You'll both have to have your memories cropped. Desmond, too, I guess. But there won't be any repercussions; you were just doing your job, too enthusiastically. You might even get a medal and not be able to remember what it was for."

Otto groped beside the bed and found the button that raised his bed to a sitting position. "How long have I been out?"

"About half a day." He checked his watch. "Fourteen hours."

"Have you been in touch with your bureau?"

"Yes . . . but I didn't tell them anything about you."

"That was smart." He straightened the tubes going into his arm and chest. "Well, let's go back to the beginning. You joined the Magdalenists eleven years ago. Were you working for BERD?"

"Yes. I was a research assistant on Earth."

"Why did they choose you?"

"I'd been a priest, a Jesuit. They shuffled some records to make it look like I was still in the order."

"All right." Otto rubbed his eyes. "This is what I don't understand. My bureau has access to everything, I mean *everything*, in Confederación files. But they didn't know about you, or Caarla, or Desmond. How is that possible?"

"I don't think I should tell you."

"Come on, now. You can either tell me everything or finish the job Caarla started. Or face brainwipe."

Applegate looked at the floor and exhaled loudly. "Well, it's simple. We only report verbally, straight to our department head. Our salaries were paid in advance, ten years' worth, and hidden in an appropriation for a new building."

Otto digested that. "Because you knew there was a Charter violation involved."

"We suspected it."

"And you're accessories to it now."

"I suppose." He looked up, defiant. "It was worth it, though. No matter what happens to us."

"You really think so."

"We got what we came for," he said. "We know now that they actually do change the planet's orbit, we know that they do it by converting matter directly to energy.

"The preliminary figures are exciting. Brother Judson took core samples from the walls in the winter room, to test for permeability. Turns out that they can process more than two kilograms of mass per hour. That's on the order of 10^{17} joules."

"I'm not a scientist. What does that mean?"

"About . . ." he gazed at the ceiling, "fifty million gigawatts. Fifty billion megawatts. Fifty trillion kilowatts. Enough to orbit a ten-ton shuttle, and then some."

"That doesn't sound like much, compared to moving a planet."

"It's enough—with a thousand of them working, they only have to do it a few minutes a day over the fifty-year dormancy."

"If all of them can do it. Balaam's says he can't."

"You can't take anything they say at face value. They removed a lot of mass from that wall, as you found out."

"What did you do about the wall?"

"Nothing permanent; we have the roof jacked up until we make a decision. Probably just let it collapse. We shouldn't need the winter room any more."

"You're stopping the experiments, of course."

"Well, that's up to the bureau—obviously, Balaam's is easier to communicate with after having been frozen and thawed out. That may be true of the others, too. If there's no Charter violation, we'll continue, but with proper equipment and a lot more funding."

Otto cocked his head at Applegate. "No Charter violation? It's *fatal!* Balaam's said he was going to die."

"That's what it said. But we checked it out with the diagnostic machine, and there's nothing wrong . . . the creature's just disoriented. Delusional."

"When is your bureau going to decide?"

"They didn't say. They had to check with Earth."

"Let me give you a piece of advice." Otto toyed with the tube leading into his chest. "Get on the side of the angels. There's a clear-cut Article Three violation here. When the dust settles, a lot of people are going to wind up in a rubber room. Or in the tank, for brainwipe. You had better act outraged, whether you are or not."

"You don't understand—"

"I understand the Charter watchdog committee. And it won't just be my testimony against you. Dr. Jones and, probably, all of her colleagues—including another TBII agent—and most of the people in this order.

"To exploit the S'kang, you'll have to demonstrate that not only will you not be harming them, but that the exploitation will result in some long-term benefit to their culture. That will be some job."

"You may underestimate my bureau."

"Bureaus." Otto laughed good-naturedly. "Let me pose for you a hypothetical situation.

"Suppose you went down the hill and searched just north of the middle of the landing strip, and found a government-issue high-powered ultraviolet laser buried there. Suppose you made an intuitive leap and decided that *I* had used that laser for TBII business, to kill that woman."

"What are you—"

"I'm talking about bureaus. Suppose you reported this homicide to your bureau. Which of us would get off this planet alive?"

"You can't threaten me."

"I think I just have."

Applegate stared at the tube. "I could reach over and—"

"You try it. I'll tear off your head and beat you to death with it." Henry flinched. "Seriously, you'd never—" A knock at the door interrupted him. Applegate unlocked it.

It was Desmond. "Henry, we've got a scrambled call from Epsilon Indii." He look at Otto. "You have a visitor. Sire."

Applegate left and Balaam's shuffled in.

"Hello, not-Joshua. Did they hurt you for trying to help me?"

"Not really. It was an accident. Besides, it doesn't look like I helped you very much."

"When you told me to go away I should have gone farther. Instinct is powerful, though; that's the place I normally stop for winter."

"I'm just sorry for you. I'll be all right, and your friends should be safe. How long do you think you have?"

"I don't know. This has never happened before. Years, probably. Ten, twenty, fifty . . . what's the difference? What can you do in fifty years?"

"Well . . . for one thing, you could help the other S'kang. Would you come back to Earth with me?"

"Is there anything to eat there? I don't think Earth insects would nourish me."

"They'd have to arrange something. It's no problem, though."

"All right. It might be interesting; besides, I won't have anyone to talk to here. Unless they wake up more."

"They won't do that. The S'kang are protected by the Charter."

"As we always were." The door opened quietly and Theo slipped in. "Prescott?" he whispered.

"Ay-firmative."

"Leave us alone for a minute, please." The S'kang went out and Theo eased the door shut. He sat down next to Otto's bed, and sighed.

"Almost over, Colonel. Your identity's spilled, but I don't think there's any harm done."

"Applegate."

"Of course. He called his supervisor on Indii. I monitored it and called our own people there. It's taken care of . . . the only people who know who you are are in this building."

"Applegate just got a call from Epsilon Indii."

"Good. They're on the job."

"You had the supervisor killed?"

"Killed or held. I left it to their discretion."

" 'Their discretion.' " Otto absorbed this, and added it to a nagging feeling. "Wait. You aren't really a Class 2 operator, you aren't Meade Johanssen."

Theo laughed. "That's right, Colonel . . . Otto. I'm Ozwald Jakobbson."

"I've heard of you. You've been a prime, what, seven or eight years?"

"Eight. Most of them here."

"No way to get rank."

"I don't know. I'm an acting colonel."

Otto shook his head. "This whole planet gives me an Alice-in-Wonderland feeling. Did they make you acting colonel so you could override me?"

"Well, I do have time-on-assignment."

"Which takes precedence over time-in-grade; I'm aware of that—"

Applegate wandered in through the door, studying a sheet of paper. He looked up suddenly. "Who are you?"

Jakobbson's hand was in his pocket. "Friend of Father Joshua's. I didn't know he was sick."

Can't tell the players without a program, Otto thought. "Theo Kutcher, Father Applegate. Theo's a Skinner Baptist from the archeologists. We've had some enjoyable arguments."

A small noise, a click, came from Jakobbson's pocket. Applegate didn't seem to hear it.

"Did he tell you what happened?" Applegate said slowly.

"Yes. Terrible accident." Jakobbson stepped to where he stood between Applegate and McGavin, at the edge of Otto's bed. He reached behind himself, as if to scratch his back, and dropped two nose filters on Otto's pillow.

Faint whiff of new-mown hay and rubber: pyrazine tetrachloride. Otto stuffed the filters in his nose.

"What was that?" Applegate leaned to look around Jakobbson. "What are you doing, Joshua?"

"Thought I had to sneeze."

"Something's going on here." Applegate drew his pocket laser and trained it on Jakobbson. "How did you get in here?"

"Walked in."

"That . . . smell . . ." Otto couldn't see, but he heard the pistol hit the floor. Then the soft thump of Applegate's heavy body. Jakobbson smiled and pulled out a remote detonator.

Otto was careful to breathe through his nose. "You put it in the central heating system?"

He nodded. "Main duct. I already took care of the archeologists. Everybody on the planet's out for at least a day."

"Paralyzed."

"Yeah, the pyrazine was all I had. I'd rather they were unconscious."

214

"What happens when they recover?"

"They'll be light years away. So will we. And as many S'kang as we can cart onto the ship."

"I'm a little behind. What ship?"

"It's a passenger liner, two hundred places." He checked his watch. "Be here in another two hours."

"A commercial liner?"

"Yes, just out of drydock. Supposedly, it's on a shakedown systems check. It'll take us to an uninhabited rock that's similar to this one. Drop us off and go back to Indii."

"Hold it." Otto tried to concentrate. His arms were tingling; must have inhaled a little of the gas. "You didn't do this with a call. It's been set up for a long time."

"Years."

"We're going to kidnap every human being on this planet, as well as about a hundred S'kang—a tenth of the population—and take them to a planet that's just as miserable as this one. Why?"

"The root reason is to keep Energia General from coming in with a billion credits and cracking the secret before the Confederación. We've kept them tied up in court for a long time, but it's just a delaying action. Harassment. E. G. will win eventually; they're using our own Charter arguments against us. They've got resources and talent, and they'll be fighting for their corporate life—"

"So they'll come here and find out that we've—"

"No, they *won't*. Not after the plague."

"Ah."

"Everyone on this world killed within a day. Confirmed by a Public Health Commission automated probe. Absolute quarantine; not even E.G. will be able to break it.

"This is where theTBII comes in—otherwise, it's a BERD project."

"Hear that, Henry?" Applegate was lying on his back, eyes open. "I told you we were on the same side."

"TBII is loaning them the specialists and equipment for memory and personality modification. The ones they don't need for continuing research, we'll repattern and—"

"Brainwipe, you mean."

"That's an ugly word, Colonel. We'll be more delicate than that."

"Sure." Otto tried to gesture but couldn't raise his arms. "Oh, hell. The tube."

"Is that thing putting air into your lung?"

"I don' know. I just work here." His legs were frozen, too.

"Well, they've got the antidote aboard the ship."

"Along with everything else, seems like. What did you need me for?"

"We had to substitute someone for Joshua. Sooner or later, he would have gotten in touch with E.G."

Scuffling sound: Balaam's lurched through the door. "Joshua? What's wrong with the air? I can't see." His eyestalks were swinging, hanging loose.

"It won't last, Prescott," Jakobbson said.

The paralysis was spreading to Otto's jaw and tongue. "Izzat true?" he whispered.

"I don't know." He shrugged. "I'm not a . . ."

Balaam's made a faint sound like a faraway siren, and settled to the floor.

After a silence, Jakobbson said, "Well, I have to go get things in order. Find their records and such. Where do they keep that computer?"

Otto tried to talk but could only make a hissing noise.

He nodded. "Guess I can find it."

For a long time Otto listened to him walking in the halls, opening and closing doors. When the sound stopped, time passed very slowly.

He watched a puddle of thin blue fluid growing from
216

under the S'kang's shell: After a while it stopped growing.

What is genocide, McGavin? You could kill ten billion humans and in a couple of generations you'd have more than you started with. Kill one S'kang and you've made a real dent.

What happens after they've used up the hundred? They come back and get another hundred. Then another hundred. Since they're immortal and can't reproduce, it isn't really genocide, not as long as one is alive. If you subtract two numbers and come up with the wrong answer, what per cent genocide is that?

Just how long, McGavin, have you known that the Charter's main function is to protect the Confederación? Not the members of the Confederación, but the organism itself. Well, the first responsibility of any organism is self-preservation. But when did you stop believing?

In a practical sense, you never did stop. You can posit and argue and posit and argue, but if the Confederación asked you to unplug yourself from that machine and die, you would unplug yourself and die, if you could move your arms. Might as well breathe through your mouth, jerk, if you get enough of it you might fall asleep.

He woke up when they loaded him and the doctor machine aboard the shuttle.

He woke up on the ship, twice, to eat.

He woke up when they were unloading the ship, dozens of big insulated containers rolled down the aisle, dormant S'kang; humans carried out on stretchers, but they didn't carry him out, and he couldn't stay awake.

He woke up for a short time moving from the big ship to a little ship, and he woke up on Earth.

INTERVIEW:
AGE 45

You understand why you have to answer these questions, don't you?

Yes, I understand, it's part of retiring

Very good. Now tell me: who was the fourteenth person you killed?

Stuart Fitz-Jones

That you remember them by number is singular. The twenty-first—who, where, and why?

That was Ajuji D'ajuji, on the planet Ojubwa, circumstantially implicated in an Article Seven violation (cybernetic penetration of international credit matrix on sister planet Fulgor), he may or may not have been guilty but he threatened me with a knife

And you killed him how?

Penlaser

Very sporting. Who was the one after him?

Benoni Jakob, same assignment, about a month later, muffed the first try and he locked himself up in a castle, I got a job in his favorite restaurant and doctored his food with an asymptomatic cumulative nerve poison, he didn't know what was happening to him, finally jumped a hundred meters onto a brick courtyard

The twenty-fifth?

Ramos Guajana, on the planet Selva, clear-cut accessory to Article

List the rest of them in order, please, just names.

Noel Duvic, D'an Foxx, Becker Conway, Beresford Sackville-West, Luanda Donner, two whose names I don't know, Yonina Dav'stern, Radomil Czerny, Reed Hitchcock, Antonio Salazar, one whose name I don't know, "Speed" Larsen, Birendra Bir Bikram, Juan Navarro, Bari: First-son-of-Marcuse, Humani Ojukwu, two natives of Corbus (they don't use names), and Joshua Immanuel in the false identity of Elizene Marietta

That's forty-five people in less than twenty years, Otto; not a record, but very high. We established yesterday that the guilt you feel for these eliminations manifests itself consciously as hostility toward the TBII and, by extension, the Confederación itself. You won't be able to adjust to retirement until you accept a more realistic view of the situation. You killed those people and you must forgive yourself, not merely shift the blame.

I understand, but you don't understand, which "me" are you talking about?

Biographical check, please, go:

I was born Otto Jules McGavin on 24 Avril AC 198, on Earth, with jus sanguinus citizenship to Karuna

That one.

That "me" died in AC 220, when he signed up for Foreign Service and you preempted him for TBII

You're evading moral responsibility by transference again.

Not true, Otto McGavin died and was replaced by what I am now, when I'm not someone else

Which is?

Something that walks and talks like Otto McGavin, and looks just like him (for what that's worth), but is mainly a construct of skills and attitudes installed by continuous hypnotic reinforcement by the TBII, between the year AC 220 and 222

That's nonsense: it's not as if you were brainwiped.

True, but there are degrees of control, the real Otto McGavin went to temple every evening and tried to follow the Eightfold Path, the construct you call Otto McGavin cheats and steals and kills for a living

But not for his own gain! He has traded the selfish pursuit of internal peace and harmony to bring peace to sentient beings throughout the Confederación.

I did believe that was true, once, but now I see how foolish, how blind I was, not seeing that the Charter is a fraud the Confederación uses to

Biographical check, please, go:

I was born Otto

Skip to age 35, please, go:

TBII liaison was a double agent, whispered the mnemonic to me just as I sat down to dinner with Patrice Becket and his bodyguards, spilled identity, had to kick table over and come up shooting, they used human shields, women and children, shooting back, I had no choice, didn't even think, really, nine dead, Christ and Buddha, the little girl's face so resigned, confused, O God, blood, spouting, all her guts sliding out in one

Skip to age 40, please, go:

Right action is abstaining from killing, stealing, and sexual

Skip to age 40, please, go:

Right livelihood is earning a living in a way not harmful to any living

Skip to age 40, please, go:

Right thought is free from lust, ill will, cruelty, and

Biographical check, please, go:

I was born, right effort is to avoid evil thoughts and overcome them

Biographical check, please, go:

Right EFfort is to aVOID evil THOUGHTS and over-COME

Biographical! Check! Please! Go!

RIGHT ACTION IS ABSTAINING FROM KILLING

Shit.

"Shit." The therapist wiggled the induction helmet off his head and tossed it clattering on the desk.

The machine operator looked up from his readout. "He looping again?"

"Yeah." He watched Otto McGavin writhing, naked and hairless, inside the tank of pale blue fluid, chin jerking as he screamed soundlessly, blind eyes staring past the wires that pierced through to the optic nerve. "Poor cob."

He patted his face with a towel and removed his outer tunic from a hook on the door. "Well, that's seven days."

"Don't you want to go the maximum?"

"No. He just gets worse."

"But he's a colonel, sir."

"That's all right: I'll take the responsibility." He started out the door.

"Wipe or waste, sir?"

"Well . . . doesn't really make much difference. I guess we've used up enough time and power. Unplug him; I'll leave a note for the clean-up crew."

MORTAL ENGINES
57406-3/$2.95

This classic collection explores the evolution of machine intelligence in 14 stories of irony, tragedy and humor. "Brilliant...a top-notch collection by one of science fiction's most articulate writers."

Chicago Daily News

THE FUTUROLOGICAL CONGRESS
58289-9/$2.75

A traveler from outer space comes to Earth for a conference, but a revolution catapults him into a synthetic future paradise created by hallucinogenic drugs.

THE CYBERIAD
51557-1/$2.50

The intergalactic capers of two "cosmic constructors" as they vie to out-invent each other building gargantuan cybernetic monsters all across the universe.

Available wherever paperbacks are sold, or directly from the publisher. Include 50¢ per copy for postage and handling; allow 6-8 weeks for delivery. Avon Books, Mail Order Dept., 224 West 57th St., N.Y., N.Y. 10019.

If you like Heinlein, will you love Van Vogt?

A READER'S GUIDE TO SCIENCE FICTION

by Baird Searles, Martin Last, Beth Meacham, and Michael Franklin

Here is a comprehensive and fascinating source book for every reader of science fiction — from the novice to the discerning devotee. Its invaluable guidance includes:

* *A comprehensive listing of over 200 past and present authors, with a profile of the author's style, his works, and other suggested writers the reader might enjoy

* *An index to Hugo and Nebula Award winners, in the categories of novel, novelette, and short story

* *An outstanding basic reading list highlighting the history and various kinds of science fiction

* *A concise and entertaining look at the roots of Science Fiction and the literature into which it has evolved today.

"A clear, well-organized introduction."
Washington Post Book World

"A valuable reference work." **Starship**